Wickea

SusuKhaa

Disclaimer

Wicked Games
Edited by: Kato Rayne
Proofread: Lottie
Formatted by: SusuKhaa
Cover by: Covers in Color
Copyright © 2021 by SusuKhaa
ISBN: 9798458813310

Storm did a bad thing...

After his father's death and he is forced to move to a remote village, Wind thinks his life is over. He's given up on a future outside of a place where the livestock outnumber the humans. That is until a full-ride scholarship offer brings him into the city and into the path of the one person he never wanted to see again.

As a teenager, Storm realized money couldn't fix everything. And every day since then, he wishes it could. Breaking Wind's heart turns out to be the worst thing he'd ever done, and he knows Wind hates him. He promises himself to make it right—but before he can, Wind and his mother disappear leaving Storm feeling empty.

Then Wind starts attending Storm's university and Storm grows a new determination.

But can Wind look away from his hatred long enough to forgive Storm? Can Wind let go and let Storm in?

Wind

The day was weirdly sunny. The sky was clear of clouds and a strange, cool breeze wrapped itself around everything.

The brightness of the day should have cheered me up. After all, I was onward to a new beginning I never thought I'd have the chance at. I was finally able to do the one thing I'd fought so hard for but had given up on once my father passed.

Why wasn't I happier?

As I stood in the courtyard, watching and feeling people swirl about me, I still felt as if my entire world was being encircled by a wall that threatened to block out the sun.

I couldn't let that happen. If the sun was gone, I'd be cold again—so cold.

My hands grew weak, and I set my baggage on the ground. Lacing my fingers, I stretched my arms above my head while pushing downward with my hips.

I moaned.

The position felt so good, I moaned again and held the stretched a little longer. When I straightened my body again, I had to duck as a ball came flying at my head.

Frowning, I glared at the girl who ran after it without apologizing for almost taking me out.

The movement of getting out of the way jarred my sore back and I wanted to cry. The journey from my village had been long. And I knew then it had worn on my body.

My mother had driven me from the village to the city, then a lengthy bus ride later, I was dropped off at a spot where the school had sent a bus to pick us up. It bounced along the street, through the downtown core and soon began dropping students off at the different campuses.

Every part of me hurt.

Still, I exhaled, stretched my entire body again then lowered my arms. I tried as best as I could to ignore the hurt, and focus on what was happening.

It had been a long time since I was around this many people. After my father's death, it took a while for my mother to find work. That forced us to move out of the city to a small, out of the way village where the livestock outnumber the humans.

The souls at the gate alone was more than the bodies in my village.

Everyone around me was happy.

How was that even possible.

It wasn't hard to tell just how excited they all were. Laughter rippled through the air as they called out to each other.

It was hard to imagine most of these people were new to the school. They were all busy hugging, chatting, smiling—they all had family and friends helping them move in.

That thought made me angry.

I was jealous.

While my mother wanted to accompany me, she couldn't. She had a job. Her boss refused to give her time off which left me struggling to get my things into my dorm.

Thankfully, there was no furniture to bring in, but I had two suitcases, a backpack and a shoulder bag with food and snacks Mae had packed for me. People pushed back and forth around me, one almost toppled me over. Gripping the suitcase handles, I steadied myself and muttered under my breath.

"Looks like you could use some help." A female voice sounded to my left.

I offered her a smile. "I'm fine." I lied. "Just need to get use to the traffic."

"Let me help." She told me.

"I don't even know your name."

"Um—" She extended a hand to me. "Gift."

I grinned and shook her hand. "Wind. Are you new too?"

"No." She replied cheerfully as she accepted my backpack and bag of food. "Second year. I had to come in early. My parents have plans on going away for a business trip and couldn't bring me in any other time."

"Oh." I dragged my suitcases up the couple of steps and used my ass to hold the door open. "At least they came with you. My mother couldn't come."

"Is she ill?"

"No. Working." I looked up for the signs leading me toward my dorm room. That led me to the elevator. "Her boss is a little bit of a jerk. He wouldn't give her the time off."

"I would have quit." Gift jabbed her finger against the button.

"She wanted to." I replied as the doors pinged open. "But I knew better. I'm okay. As long as she is here for my graduation, I'm good."

"Seems like a good trade."

On the fifteenth floor, we exited the lift and according to the numbers on the wall, we had to go right. I found my admission letter and double checked the dorm room number.

When I managed to get the door open, I was stunned at the size of it. I would be sharing it with one other student, but even so, it was larger than I expected.

When my mother and I toured the dorms months before, they were entirely too small, causing my mother to worry.

Arching a brow, I set the suitcases to the side, accepted the bags from Gift then looked around.

"Your room is huge." Gift oohed. "How did you swing this? I can't even turn around without crashing into my roommate."

"I have no idea, P." I managed while walking over to the window to lookout.

The view was off trees, lush and green for as far as the eyes could see. In the distance, the very far distance, tall buildings towered upward, and I imagined how beautiful the lights would look at nights.

I exhaled, I turned to look at the space again.

The space was set up for convenience and to use every bit of ground they could.

As we stepped through the front door, it was into an alley kitchen. Moving deeper, it opened into a small dining space and to the left was the bedroom and a small area with a sofa.

The bedroom had two of everything.

Two beds.

Two desks and chairs with cute little lamps and an empty rack for books.

The walls were bare but across the room from the foot of the beds were two wardrobes. A closed door further in caught my attention and I assumed that was the bathroom.

"It's nice though." Gift took her turn looking out the window. "I'm jealous."

"I'm pretty sure it's just because of my scholarship, P." I told her as I rummaged through the snacks.

Producing two bags of potato chips, I handed one to Gift. She hesitated for a moment as she muttered something about getting fat but eventually indulged.

"I'm trying to be good with the junk food." She admitted. "I gained a little weight over the summer break."

I blinked. "Where?" I asked.

She was thin. If she turned sideways, she'd probably disappear.

I still didn't understand what she meant about being fat.

4

Gift shrugged and shoved a chip into her mouth. "I see it when I take off my clothes."

"Trust me, P. You're not fat—ugh, I'm so nervous right now."

"Why?" She looked around.

"I'm not used to this." I admitted. "And I have to share this room with someone else."

Gift sighed dramatically. "I'm sure it'll be fine. I was scared to sleep in the same place with a stranger too. I'm not sure if anyone thinks of that before they force us to co-exist like this. But for the most part, it's safe."

"For the most part?" I choked on some chips. "That's not reassuring."

"It's fine." Gift laughed. "I'm sure it's fine."

I sputtered and shook my head. "We should change the subject. You suck at this."

Gift chuckled. "Sorry. Not used to having close friends—not that I'm saying—how did your mother take you moving?"

I thought back to my mother. She'd smiled after she'd hugged me right before I climbed onto the bus for the long ride away from home.

Though she'd smiled, I could see the sadness in her eyes. They told me she'd cried the entire night and I had been helpless to prevent it.

I couldn't help wondering how differently our lives would have been if my father hadn't gotten sick? If he'd listened and gone to see a doctor when my mother and I begged him to. But he was worried about the cost—I would have happily gone without a few meals just to make sure he was diagnosed on time and treated.

I was her only child, the only company she really had since my father's death.

Though she'd developed friends in the village, my mother and I were close, we took care of each other.

"She wasn't happy." I admitted. "But mothers sacrifice their own happiness for their children all the time. She knows this is best for me. And I love her for it. I just hope I can make something out of myself to repay her for the sadness moving away brings on her."

"I'm sure you make her happy now."

"Maybe." I rolled the open edge of the chip bag and set it on my desk. The saltiness irritated me.

"How did you manage moving on your first day?"

"So-so." Gift replied. "My mother brought me since my father was working. There wasn't really any fanfare. But I wasn't scared. My parents would send me to international camps when I was a kid. Living away from home wasn't new."

"International camps?"

Gift nodded. "Yeah—English camps mostly. They wanted me to be able to speak English. They thought it would give me a leg up when I took over the family business."

I tilted my head.

"My parents own a series of highly successful hotels in Switzerland, Japan and England. Never mind that I don't want to go into business."

"What's your major?"

'To my parents' horror—Dramatic Arts."

I chuckled. "That will give you zero training to run hotels."

"Precisely." Gift crumpled the empty snack pack into a fist and dropped it into the garbage. "Right now, they are going with it secretly hoping I'll either fail or change my mind. Hence the need to remain in shape."

I sighed and took another look around the room. The size of it still shocked me. This space would be a better space for a senior—it made no sense.

Gift smiled. "We should exchange LINE."

Though I was curious as to why, I accepted her LINE and offered my own. I was new to the school and didn't really have a history of making friend easily.

6

The truth was, I was a year behind the students my age as I took a year off between high school and university. My mother wasn't in a good place for me to leave her. I didn't want to depend on others, mostly strangers, to care for her as I jetted off for any reason.

I took the year off and as it drew to a close, I figured I would just forget going to university all together. That is until the letter came in the mail explaining that they knew I was a good student, and it wasn't beneficial to Thailand should my mind go without training.

I had rolled my eyes then, but my mother was overjoyed at this chance.

Gift invited me to the festivals that night and while I wasn't a big fan of large gatherings of people, I happily agreed.

I wasn't sure what it was about crowds, but since we moved to the village, I was just happier on my own.

Gift offered me a thumbs up before all but skipping out the door. I watched her go then shook my head and dragged my palms along my jean-clad thighs, wondering what to do with myself.

Tightness in my chest pushed me to sit on one of the beds. I took slow, deep breaths to control the race of my heart and the light-headedness the panic caused. The silence of the room forced me to face the fact with what I had done.

I had to face the idea that when I climbed into bed in a few hours, my mother wouldn't be down the hall, that I wouldn't hear the chirps of cricket outside my window or be able to hang half my body out the window to wave at neighbours.

I was no longer in a small village where everyone protected and cared for me.

I couldn't melt into my mother's hugs when the day became too much. Her arms were the only place I had known comfort, kindness, and I'd lost the convenience of a mother's love.

To take my mind off the panic in my head, I set to task choosing my bed, packing out my things and putting away my very little clothing in the wardrobe at the foot of my bed.

I didn't have much—unpacking hadn't taken long.

To further calm myself down, I showered, changed into a pair of blue jeans and a white dress shirt.

Feeling much better, I climbed into bed and called my mother.

"Are you alright?" Mae asked.

"I'm okay, Mae." I told her. "I have all my things settled—my desk packed out. I have to buy another sheet set though. I can do that tomorrow."

"Didn't you take the one I offered?"

"Mae, I told you." I sighed. "You need that for your bed. I have a little money saved up, so it won't be a problem. Don't worry."

"Let me know if you need more." She told me. "I have some fabric and can make you some."

"I won't need sheets right now. But I'll take a blanket."

Mae laughed. "Okay, my love. Have you met your roommate yet?"

I shook my head needlessly. "Not yet. It's strange they hadn't sent me the information on him, right? All I know is that he's a music major and is in a band."

"Don't overthink it." She laughed softly. "It's probably a mistake. Now, did you put the food in the fridge? I know you can't eat all of it at once."

"The snacks are in my drawer at my desk." I replied. "Everything else is in the fridge."

She quizzed me for a while longer before she was called to get back to work. I felt bad for her—I wanted to be able to make it, so she didn't have to work so hard anymore.

Since my father's death, she'd had to work very hard to raise me.

Even after I found a job myself, things were still hard for us.

Before hanging up, I quickly reminded her of my love for her.

"I love you too." Her voice trembled and I knew she'd be crying again the moment she could.

Sighing, I hung up and flopped backward to my pillows.

But I was restless, and after gathering my wallet from where it was in the side of my backpack, I left the dorm to wander the campus.

It seemed I was inside long enough for all the students to move in. The campus now felt like one from a BL drama. There were students sitting under trees, others cycling along concrete paths and a few clouds had drifted in overhead.

Giving myself my second tour of the place, I wound up in the canteen.

After ordering some food, I sat alone at a table to eat. By the time I was finished, I still didn't know what to do with myself. I wandered around until I found myself in the library where I stayed, reading until I received a text from Gift trying to figure out where I was.

Setting the book back where I found it, I replied to her message to tell her I was on my way and scrambled from the building.

I asked directions from students I met along the way and soon, found Gift playing about on her phone. When she saw me, she put it away, took my hand and we set off on going through the festival that was slowly picking up.

"Don't tell me all these students are new." I spoke close to her ear.

"Of course not." She high-fived a passing student who had writing all over his clothes and face. "Some are seniors."

"Seniors?"

"Yeah. They are out to welcome all the nongs."

Someone began playing the drums and Gift shoved both her hands in the air and cheered.

I laughed.

9

"Have some fun, N'Wind!" She bounced me with her hip. "Woo!"

I still wasn't a fan of crowds, but I focused on what was happening around us, outside of the crowds.

Everyone was friendly, stopping to drape flowers around my neck and a crown of flowers around Gift's head. She giggled as we both offered the senior wai and continued on.

From time to time, we stopped to dance to music being played by a group of students, to wiggle our bodies to the beautiful drumming by another or the strangely haunting tune of a clarinet.

Booths were set up around the large school yard. We stopped at one after the other picking up little giftbags, snacking on sweets and trying to figure out what club I wanted to join. I had three in mind, the film club, the soccer team or Muay Thai.

I had done lot of acting in high school, auditioning for all the school plays and the one school film our high school ever put on.

I knew nothing of Muay Thai and could only play one song on the guitar.

But I figured I could learn.

At the bonfire, seniors tied white or red strings around the juniors' wrists, wishing them luck and success in their studies and beyond.

Gift tied one around my wrist, since she was my senior and we wandered off to a nearby noodle stand.

We could still hear the music and happiness coming from the festival as we slurped noodles into our mouths. The excitement to storm through me was new. I had never been to anything like this before.

Though for the first part of my life, we lived in a big enough city to have one, after my father's death, we had to move away to a remote village in order to survive.

It was cheaper, even with my mother driving back and forth between the city and our village.

At first, I hated it.

But after a while, I actually grew to love it.

We finished our meals and went back to the festivities. As we danced along with everyone else, I turned to accept a bottle of water the seniors had been handing out. I came face to face with the one person I never wanted to see again.

It was stunning how quickly my emotions changed.

How my happiness grew black with my anger and hatred.

Though I tried controlling it, I had no control over the way my feet launched me forward. Without warning, I swung on him hitting him hard across the face.

Gift gasped and grabbed my arm while one of his friends stepped forward as if to protect him. He lifted a hand and his friend backed off, but I didn't care.

I hated him.

I wanted him dead—I'd dreamt of him getting hit by lightning.

A few times I'd imagined wrapping my fingers around his throat and squeezing until there was nothing left.

"Apologize." Gift demanded. "You can't hit your senior like this. Say you're sorry."

"Over my dead body!" I snapped at her. "He doesn't deserve to be respected as my senior! He doesn't deserve anything good—not now, not ever! I'll not apologize!"

To stress my point, I shrugged from her grasp and stormed off. My rage pulsed through me like and overwhelming dark cloud.

Gift caught me under a large tree leading toward the gates.

"What did you do?" Gift asked. "You can't just walk up and punch a senior in the face!"

"He had it coming, P!" I told her. "He's selfish and spoiled and I hate him!"

"Nong."

"I will *not* apologize until he can bring my father back."

"What?"

"Nothing, P. I'd like to be alone now." I told her and stormed off again.

Though I wasn't sure where I was going, I continued walking until when I looked up, all I saw were small houses around me. I sat on the sidewalk, buried my face in my hands and allowed the tears to roll down my cheeks.

I thought I had left all of that behind—the pain of that day, the absolute helplessness. I had been a good son, listened to my mother, still paid tribute to my father but still I was being punished for some sins I couldn't seem to remember.

Of all the schools he could have gone to, off all the campuses he could have chosen, he chose this one. I didn't have a choice in where I went. I didn't have the money he did. He could have studied a broad, gone to Bangkok—Narnia, anywhere.

Why here?

I dried my cheeks and rested backward on my palms to look up at the sky as my phone vibrated in my pocket. It was Gift—it had to be. I didn't want to talk to her. She was probably trying to get me to say I was sorry for what I had done.

I wasn't sorry.

I'd do it again.

Usually, I wasn't a violent person. I went out of my way to avoid fights. But for some reason when it came to him, all I wanted to do was punch him until there was nothing left.

I stayed where I was seated in the silence of the strange neighbourhood for a while longer then made my way back in the direction I'd travelled earlier.

Somehow, I made it back to the university that was now eerily silent.

I skirted the outer edges of the campus, only cutting across along a path that led through a row of trees then wound up in front of the dorm.

It dawned on me then that I would be spending the next three years there.

I sighed helplessly, crossed the parking lot and entered the front doors five minutes before curfew.

The lobby was quiet, so was the ride up the elevator. The only sound once I excited was my heart rumbling in my chest and the clop of my shoes on the tiled floor.

I let myself in the doors but almost tumbled over a bag. Frowning, I used my foot to ease it out of the way.

-The bathroom door opened then and out stepped Klahan Bannarasee—some dope in his family decided to call him Storm.

What have I done to deserve this?

Storm

Standing in front of the bathroom mirror, I looked at my face while opening my mouth as wide as I could to work out the soreness Wind's punched had caused. Anyone else did that would be on the ground being beaten to death. But with Wind, I understood his anger, his rage.

I'd caused it.

Sure, I knew he'd be angry, but this—this was new.

Exhaling loudly, I went back to unpack, putting my clothes away, setting up my desk and tossing my snack packs into my desk drawer. I was just about to shove my suitcase underneath my bed when my phone buzzed. Kneeling on the floor, I pulled it out and sighed.

"Practice tonight?" Kai asked in his text.

"Yeah. I booked the room for seven." I replied.

"I'll see you there." Kai replied. "I'm going with Gear to the mall. We will be back with enough time."

"Cool."

Setting the phone on the desk, I refocused my attention to the suitcase. It barely fit under the bed, but at least it was out of the way.

I'd spent the summer break with my grandfather and brother. I'd worked in my grandfather's company during that time as well as grew old enough to inherit a large fortune from my grandmother.

People around me thought I was a fool to continue with school—but I'd always been taught by my grandfather that money came and went. Education, he said, lasted forever.

Curious, I went through his things—looking through his closet to see he didn't have much clothes there.

Two pairs of black pants and two pristinely clean and pressed white shirt. He only had one black tie to go with the uniform that the university required.

Aside from those, he had a couple pairs of jeans, pair of trackpants and a quite a few graphic shirts that ranged from Pink Floyd to *Death Note.*

I found his snack horde that included chocolate bars, quite a few with coconut, snack bars, chips and a bag of assorted candies.

It seemed Wind had a sweet-tooth.

Noticing the time going, I knew I had to focus on the work at hand. I still had to finish a song for my band for the season since our fans had heard everything we have in our arsenal already. I had chosen love song—something different than what we had before, and I hoped people wouldn't frown at it and not want anything to do with us.

I'd just finished hauling on my clothes and was drying my hair while exiting the bathroom when he entered the room.

Seeing me for the second time that day didn't seem to help his mood any.

I didn't have to ask if he was happy to see him.

He was seething.

"Get out!" Wind pointed to the door. "How did you even get in here?"

"I live here."

"You can't be my roommate!"

"And yet, I am your roommate." I countered.

"What did I do in a previous life to be this cursed?" Wind asked dramatically. "What did I do?"

"I'm not a curse, Wind."

He glared at me. "What are you doing here?"

I sighed. "I go to school here. I'm in the music program."

"You could have gone to any university you wanted." Wind pointed out.

"Not every other university has what I need."

"Anywhere in the world." Wind continued as if I hadn't spoken. "Why are you here haunting me? Why here?"

"Because they have the best music program."

"You're lying."

"I've been here for two years already, Wind." I tossed my hands up. "If anything, you followed me here."

He scoffed.

"I'm not leaving because you're uncomfortable with my presence. So, you're going to have to deal with it."

Wind frowned at him, climbed into his bed, and pulled the sheets over his head.

I went to work on my band's new song, snacking on some gummy worm candies until it was time for me to head to the campus for practice with my band.

By the time I walked into the room, I was exhausted. The colour in my cheek had become a slight dark colour.

"I don't understand why you just took that." Seua adjusted the stool behind his drum set. "He hit you."

"It's fine." I grumbled.

"Trust us, Storm knows he had that hit coming." Kai pointed out.

I said nothing.

"I'm surprised it's taken N'Wind this long." Kai continued.

"You know that kid?" Seua asked.

I nodded. "I brought what I have of the song so far. It's finished but I'm not completely happy with it."

My friends exchanged looks as I changed the subject, but neither of them questioned it.

"*Remember Fireflies.*" Seua read the title.

"We'll try it." Kai promised. "I'm sure it's not that bad."

Though I wasn't in the mood for music, I couldn't let my friends down. We worked through the song, and it was evident it was choppy and needed plenty of work.

"I probably need to write something else." I confided after we tried playing through the song twice. "I don't know anything about love."

"Yeah, you do." Kai told me. "

"Don't." I warned.

Seua arched a brow. "What are you guys not telling me?"

"Nothing." I grumbled, while packing up my guitar. "I have to go. I'll have something better for next practice. I can't concentrate right now."

"I love this song." Seua told me. "You just have to rework a couple of things. Trust me—it has good bones. Promise me you'll work on it."

I sighed and met his eyes.

"Promise me." Seua pushed. "I want to use it in the film."

Added pressure—great.

I nodded and after hugging my friends, I let myself out the backdoor and headed back to the dorms. When I let myself in, Wind was in the same position I'd left him in—facing the wall, the sheet over his head.

Saying nothing, I set my guitar down, showered then snacked on a bar and some water.

It was late.

Exhausted, I climbed into bed and shifted to my back to stare up at the ceiling. Sleep didn't come, and there I was, stretched out, watching dark shadows move across the ceiling. The Shadows vanished slowly as the moon rose higher and higher into the sky.

By the time I woke up the next morning, I was alone. Wind was gone, his bed made, and his desk neatly stacked.

Shaking my head, I unplugged my cell from the charger and climbed out of bed. After haphazardly throwing the sheets over it, I showered, dressed and left to face the day of classes.

The first half of my morning, I spent alone. I had no classes with Kai which I was thankful for.

I knew my friend was worried and he'd have a bunch of questions I had no answers for or didn't want to find answers for.

But I couldn't ignore him at lunch.

I was hoping to get there first to have a few minutes to kind of exhale. But I wasn't that lucky because when I got there, my friends were already there with my little brother, Gear.

"P!" Gear immediately shifted so I could sit beside him.

When I did, I rested my head on his shoulder for a quick second. "Want me to get you something to eat?"

"No, I got it." I promised.

After greeting Seua and Kai, I went to get something to eat then returned to my spot beside my brother.

"I pushed my food around on my plate. The others talked among themselves around me, but I couldn't seem to focus on them and their talk.

"Hey, P." My baby brother Gear snapped his fingers in front of my eyes. "Are you okay?"

I sighed. "I was thinking about the song." It wasn't exactly a lie—

Okay, fine, it was partially a lie.

Mostly, a lie.

"What were you thinking?" Seua asked.

"Well, right now, it's about falling in love." I leaned in to meet their eyes. "What if I changed it to a guy who is already in love but the person, he loves doesn't return the feelings?"

"Unrequited love.' Kai was nodded. "You might have to change the tempo."

"I can do that." I told them. "I mean—it could work, right?"

Seua nodded. "I like that."

Hearing that gave me a new lease on the song.

I pulled out my notebook and a pen and began reworking the song.

At one point, an overwhelming feeling pulsed through me, forcing me to look up. It was in time to see Wind and a female enter the canteen. They were in a deep conversation but the moment our eyes met, Wind set his tray in a nearby table, turned on his heels and left the canteen with the girl calling after him.

Shaking my head, I went back to the song, cleaned it up some and handed it to Seua as I rose and picked up my bag.

"I'm leaving." I told them.

"You haven't really eaten anything, P." Gear pointed out.

"I'm not hungry." I replied. "You can give me back the book later."

Before Kai, Gear or Seua could speak again, I was already halfway toward the door Wind had exited through mere moments before.

When I stepped into the hall, he was nowhere to be found, neither was his friend. I assumed she was his girlfriend from the way she was clinging to him when they entered.

Tossing my bag over one shoulder, I made my way to my next class and went through the rest of my day, feeling as if the worse thing in life was sitting on my shoulders.

Back at the dorm, Wind wasn't there. Even after I delayed myself, packing my gym bag slower than I usually would, he still hadn't returned.

Even when I tossed the bag over my shoulder and exited the room, heading to Muay Thai, he was still not there.

I knew what that meant.

Wind was avoiding me.

Two hours later, after every part of me ached and I returned to our room—he wasn't back.

He walked into the room about a minute before curfew, showered and climbed right into bed. Sitting up, I figured he'd want to say something—explain where he'd been, tell me how he felt now, anything.

He didn't.

I waited, even though a part of me knew he wouldn't pay me any attention.

Wind plugged his phone in to charge, rolled to face the wall away from me and pulled the sheet up to his shoulder.

I said nothing to him—I wasn't sure why his absence made me so angry, or why seeing that girl pawing all over him made me want to scream.

Flopping back to my pillow, I pushed a gust of air out my mouth and stared up at the ceiling.

When I woke again, Wind was gone.

"Shit." I swore and dragged a finger across my phone's screen to stop the alarm.

It would be a long, hot day.

Seua had volunteered me to help him and Kai with the film club's booth at the club days. It was when the juniors chose what clubs they would join to get points for graduation. I'd manage to get Wind off my mind when I looked up to see his girlfriend dragging him toward our booth.

I frowned and meant to walk away but Kai was blocking me on one side and Seua on the other. Not wanting to make a scene, I remained where I stood, watching him carefully without speaking.

The girl offered wai which I begrudgingly returned.

"My name is Gift-kha." She explained. "I'm not a junior but I didn't join any clubs last year. I was wondering if I could sign up."

Though I wanted to tell her to go away, I nodded and handed her the form. I also handed one to Wind which he promptly ignored.

"Don't be rude." Gift bounced him gently with her hip.

Instead of apologizing, Wind stormed off and I climbed over the table and followed with Kai yelling after me.

When I finally was able to catch his arm, he shrugged away from me and whirled around, anger blazing in his eyes.

"What is your problem?" I demanded?

Wind shoved my chest angrily. "You!" He snapped. "You're my problem! I hate you! You hear me? I *hate* you."

Before I could gather myself, to get over the shock of those words, he was already walking off and disappearing around the side of the building. I glanced around to see if anyone had seen what had just happened.

I was alone.

Relieved, I covered my face with one hand then dragged the same one up my face and through my hair.

I hate you!

Those words stabbed me in the chest, left me breathless and speechless. It took me a little while to gather myself.

I used the time to wander to a nearby café and picked up enough snacks and cold drinks for myself and friends then returned to the table.

"You okay?" Kai wanted to know.

"Fine." I grunted, handing him the tray with the drinks on it. "Why do you ask?"

Kai took his favorite and handed the other to Seua then proceeded to look through the bag I brought back.

"Nong Wind came back." Kai replied. "He did not look impressed. Aside from the fact the two of you don't have a very good past, I remembered that first day he walked up and punched you in the face. Want to tell me what's going on between the two of you now? Maybe I can help."

"Trust me—other than what you already know, there's nothing you can do to help. I'm his roommate."

"You're his what?" Kai asked. "I'm sure you had something to do with that."

"Don't be dumb." I slurped from the straw. "Did he at least sign up for the club?"

"Reluctantly." Seua told me. "His friend talked him into it. I think he did it more to shut her up than because he really wanted to. I wouldn't count on him and probably should add an extra member to the group—just in case."

I grunted.

By the time club day was over, I was exhausted.

I knew going back to the dorm would do no good for me to get it together.

All I wanted to do was go to my grandfather's place and crawl into bed after a bowl of his very delicious congee.

Still, the others insisted on going out for dinner and I was left seated at a noisy table, stabbing pork with my fork.

"You're really quiet, P." Gear pointed out in a whisper. "What's wrong?"

"I'm just tired." I lied.

That answer seemed acceptable as my baby brother rubbed my back for a bit then used his spoon to put some peas onto my plate.

Ever since he as a kid, he never liked green peas and took every chance he got to sneak them onto my plate.

I never scolded him for it, and I never gave away his secret.

Now that he was older, I smiled and scooped them into my mouth with my fork.

I ate so the others wouldn't ask questions.

Seua laughed at something Kai said. I smiled but I didn't hear the joke.

The two of then built a friendship fairly quickly. While Kai and I knew each other since childhood, we met Seua in our first year when he was looking to join a band.

If we were to be honest, he was looking for a place to belong since his parents had abandoned him when he was only a baby.

When he told me his story, it had angered me. His parents didn't deserve him.

Despite my mode, dinner was good and as we congregated outside to say goodbye, Kai offered to drop Gear back to his apartment.

I nodded, hugged Gear, then bumped fists with Kai.

Seua and made our way back to my car. His dorm was next to mine and since he didn't have his new car yet, I was taking him around as much as I could.

If I couldn't drive, I'd just hand him my keys.

"I love what you did with the reworked song." Seua admitted as we hit the road. "A song is supposed to make you feel something, you know?"

"Mmm." I replied.

"The chorus is what really gets me."

I smiled. "So, we're good with it now?"

"More than."

"Is this song about some real-life experience?" Seua asked.

"Partially."

It was only a half truth.

The pain I put in the song was real.

There was nothing like being in love with someone for a long time—for so long it felt like an eternity, only to find out they would never love you back.

Not even a little bit.

"You don't have to tell me." Seua's voice was soft. "But with my background, I don't think I'll ever find someone to love me. I'm bad luck."

"Seua…"

"I know what people whisper when I walk by." He cut me off. "You don't have to protect me from that. Just know being able to love someone—even if they don't love you back, is kind of a blessing. I can't even let myself do that."

"You'll find someone, Seua. And it'll be when you least expect it."

"Can I tell you a secret?"

I nodded.

"You can't tell anyone—not even Gear or P'Kai."

23

"I promise."

"I've never been with anyone."

I glanced over at him as he bowed his head.

"No one?" I asked. "Not even a kiss?"

Seua shook his head. "There was one—well, apparently, I'm afraid of intimacy."

"All of us are."

"But you've been out—like on a date."

"I've dated." He continued. "But the moment they hear about where I come from—anyway. All I'm trying to say is, don't be too hard on yourself and don't let this person not loving you back force you to close yourself up to the possibilities of others. Sometimes that person just isn't the right one."

I smiled. "Thanks, Seua."

"Of course." He patted my shoulder. "What are brothers for?"

"Precisely."

We weren't really brothers. But I remembered telling him that Kai and I would adopt. I meant it, especially with the friendship we'd developed over the years.

The memory made me smile again.

"I was thinking of writing a second one." I admitted, trying to change the subject. "Something fun to kind of counter the darkness of the first."

Seua laughed. "I'll agree to that. A band can't have too many tricks up its sleeves."

I agreed and Suea pulled out my notebook and placed it on the seat behind his back.

I promised him I would keep tweaking the song as I dropped him off. He reached across and patted my shoulder, wished me good night and climbed from the passenger side of my car.

I waited until he was inside the building. It was a habit of mine, just to make sure the person was safe. I then eased my vehicle across the lot to park between a Bugatti and a Honda.

For a moment, I paused to catch my breath.

After gathering my bag and notebook, I was reaching for the door handle when someone familiar pushed through the glass doors and descended the steps toward the parking lot.

I blinked and realized it was Gift and my heart instantly fell.

She was with Wind, alone in our room.

Suddenly, my mind took on all kinds of things they could have been doing—all of them made me sick.

It only became worse when Wind came running out the door, waving a piece of material in his hand. She laughed and accepted it, glanced around then shoved it into her bag.

The two hugged and I couldn't stand to watch anymore.

I closed my eyes, praying when I opened them again, it would be over.

Thankfully, when I did, the parking lot and the entrance to the dorms were empty. I wandered up to the room, wanting a shower and go to sleep but Wind was agitated. He pointed to a pair of my trackpants.

"Keep your things on your side of the room." He told me simply.

"We're sharing the room." I told him. "I can put my things where I want."

"That's not how it works!" He snapped, glaring at me. "You keep your space clean and tidy, and I do the same. You keep your dirty laundry where they're supposed to be kept, I do the same thing! It is not that hard! You may have servants at home, but I'm not your servant and this is not your home!"

"You're being—"

Wind picked up his phone and left.

I wasn't finished arguing with him yet, but I was too tired to really go after him. I figured, I'd take a shower, then worked on *Remember Fireflies* until he returned.

But staying up all night did no good.

Wind did not come back until early in the morning just before he was schedule to wake up for classes.

"Where have you been?" I demanded. "You don't just break curfew."

Wind turned to look at me with his head tilted to one side. "You're not my mother."

"I'm your senior and I'm sick of you disrespecting me, N'Wind!" I barked.

"My senior?" He scoffed. "That's rich."

Wind reached for his towel and was heading toward the bathroom when I caught him by the arm and spun him to face me.

"This conversation isn't over." I told him, easing in close. "Where were you?"

"I could have been at a friend's, or in the middle of Patpong." He growled at me. "My whereabouts last night is still none of your business, *P*."

I was stunned into angry silence.

"That enough respect for you?"

Angry, I pushed away from him, and Wind locked himself into the bathroom.

I could barely breathe—I was furious.

Wind

When I woke the next morning, Storm was still asleep. He didn't have his first class until after lunch. But since I didn't know what time, he went to bed the night before, he was probably still tired.

While he slept, I stood over him, looking down at his peaceful face, wondering how he was so different while he was awake.

The sheet had fallen to his hips exposing a muscular chest with dark pink nipples.

I licked my lips but forced my eyes to travel downward from an impressive six pack to the part of his frame that sloped down into a perfect waist.

Just beneath his navel was a thin line of dark hair that was strangely attractive.

I wanted to touch him there, to drag my tongue along it, up or down—I didn't care the direction.

"What's wrong with me?" I whispered.

Catching myself, I rooted round in my closet for a clean towel then ran into the bathroom closing the door behind me, trying to calm my breathing.

I ran the water for a while, trying to get the right temperature that I needed.

It quickly dawned on me, that it wasn't going to do what I wanted.

Impatiently, I shook my hand underneath the downpour, waiting.

The water in the shower hadn't been cold enough, but I managed to get my body to behave long enough to shower, dry my body and dressed.

When I stepped out of the bathroom, Storm was awake, sitting up and rubbing the sleep from his eyes.

"What?" Storm asked.

"Huh?"

"You're staring." He pointed out. "Something wrong?"

"Um—no—I mean—"

Storm stared at me for a bit then shrugged and climbed out of bed. I averted my eyes—it was partially not to see anything that my might shifted in his boxers during the night and partly out of guilt that I had stared at him the way I had.

"I have to go."

Quickly, I grabbed my bag and rushed out the door to face my day.

But instead of paying attention in class, I found myself sketching his headless torso instead of taking notes.

At one point, the teacher almost caught me, but I managed to turn the page before she arrived at my desk.

My heart raced, almost painfully, as I tried clearing my mind.

After class, I stopped to pick up some snacks, then darted across campus to meet up with Gift. I couldn't be late as she was donating her time to help me.

"I brought snacks, P!" I told her once I settled down beside her in the grass.

"Really?" She accepted the bag and peered in. "I've been laying off sugar and now I'm craving it."

"Isn't it better to just cut back on sugar rather than cutting it out completely?" I asked, pulling my books from my bag so we could get started.

"Stop agreeing with my doctor." Gift pouted prettily.

I laughed and shook my head.

We got to work, but I couldn't understand anything she was saying.

I had a test coming up, and I couldn't seem to focus much.

It'd been two days since I argued with Storm, two days and other than asking me why I had been staring, he hadn't said a word to me.

Deep down, I really thought that was what I wanted—for him to leave me alone. But as he moved around me in the room, I couldn't help feeling horrible about the things I'd said to him.

True, I didn't like him.

He was too rich for his own good and he'd used that wealth to rob me of something I held dear. Then, he tried tossing money at me, hoping I'd go away, like a few Bahts were going to change the fact I wanted him dead.

But I had been rude to him that night.

That whole thing about Patpong was uncalled for.

I wasn't sure what it was about him that brought such a petty person out in me.

"You're not paying attention!" Gift said for what had to be the millionth time. "Your test is tomorrow!"

I sighed, closed my eyes and lifted my face to the cool breeze as the leaves whispered around us. I'd asked her to tutor me for the test since she'd taken the course the year before.

I was ruining it.

"*Kho tod, P.*" I managed when I met her eyes again.

"What is going on with you?" She wanted to know. "You've been distracted."

"I'm just—I'm worried."

"About?"

"This will be my first test in university." I told her. "I mean, I took a year off schooling. What if I'm no good at it?"

Gift shook her head.

"Just because you took a year off," she said. "Doesn't mean you stop being a good student. You were obviously amazing why they hunted you down and gave you a full ride to come here. They see something in you, so stop putting yourself down and pay attention."

Exhaling, I cleared my throat and nodded. "Show me how to work this equation again."

Gift nodded and we both hunched over the problem once more time with fresh eyes. We worked through all the examples until I was in a good place then Gift suggested we stopped and focus on something else before our brains exploded.

I agreed.

After we finished classes for the day, I met her in the Dramatic Arts building and we made our way into the theatre for the first meeting of the film club.

That too made me nervous.

It'd been well over a year since I'd done any acting and I was never in front of a camera before. Everything I'd done was for the stage—but because of their caseload, the stage students did not have time for clubs.

Therefore, no drama club.

When we entered, only Kai, Seua and Gear were in attendance so far. It seemed like Gear would be the photographer for the actual club.

"I wonder where P'Storm is?" Gift asked.

I was curious too, but I merely grunted at her question as we found seats close to the front. A few others entered after us and soon Seua cleared his throat, offered us wai and looked around the room.

"Thank you all for coming." He began. "As you know, though we are a club, they expect a movie by the end of the semester. This year, I was asked to write something LGBT+ in celebration of PRIDE. I have a romantic comedy in mind."

I glanced at Gift, unsure of how I felt about a Rom Com.

"What's wrong?" Gift whispered.

"Nothing." I lied.

"It has a very nice love story to carry it." Seua continued. "The paper P'Kai is handing out is the information for auditions—including the roles and the like. I will be giving members of this club the first chance to audition and if we can't find someone suitable for the roles, we open it up to outsiders."

Once I received the sheet of paper, I couldn't seem to focus on anything else. I did love acting—maybe this was the perfect thing I needed to keep my mind off Storm.

"Are you going to audition?" Gift whispered to me.

"Yeah, P." I replied. "I like the description for Dae."

"You do know there will be kissing."

"It's only pretend, right?"

Gift giggled. "I hope you get it and the guy you have to kiss is gorgeous."

I blushed but I secretly hoped so too.

At the end of the meeting, when only myself, Gift, Kai and Gear remained behind with Seua, I asked to speak with him in private.

"P'Seua, I'd like to sign up to audition." I told him.

Seua arched a brow. "Does that mean you're staying in the club?"

I nodded. "Why wouldn't I?"

"Didn't you sign up under duress?"

My cheeks heated and I sighed. "I know, but I'd still like to sign up…"

Seua rested a hand on his hip and nodded. "But?"

"Well, I've acted before—but nothing anything like this." I admitted. "And I'm sure acting for camera is much different than for the stage. What do I even use as an audition piece?"

Seua smiled warmly. "Nong, don't put so much stress on yourself. Rewatch your favorite romantic comedies and find monologues from them. Or…"

He stopped to pull a page from his notebook and began scribbling on it. When he was finished, he handed me the page.

"Go to any one of these websites. You should be able to find something appropriate."

I accepted the paper with both hands, offered him wai then folded the paper. "Thank you, P."

Gift and I left the room and we headed toward the exit. Storm entered then but I looped my arm with Gift's and walked by him as if I didn't see him. When we climbed into Gift's car to head for dinner, she had questions.

"What's going on between you and P'Storm?" Gift wanted to know.

"It's a long story." I told her, not wanting to talk about it.

"You can't keep being rude to him." She told me. "If you do that in front of other seniors or teachers, you'd be in so much trouble."

"Don't stand up for him." I snapped. "Don't let the face fool you, P'Gift. He's not a good person."

"P'Storm!"

I blinked to refocus on what was happening in time to see Gift climbing out of the car. She jogged over to where Storm was standing, one hand in his pocket and his bag over one shoulder. The two of them went into a conversation, with Gift giggling and bowing her head as if she was blushing.

Seeing her with him like that made me mad.

Why did he have to flirt with her?

Before I could get another thought in, the two of them approached the car, Storm climbed in behind her and she pulled her slender body back behind the wheel.

"P'Storm is coming to dinner with us." She announced happily. "It's about time we all have a nice sit down."

I gripped the seat between my legs as she started the ignition. I held onto it so tightly, my nails sank through the soft leather. When we arrived at the restaurant, Gift left us outside the door to see if she could score us a table. The truth was, we should have booked a reservation.

Then again, Gift and her family were wealthy. Getting a table shouldn't be an issue.

"Did you really have to invite yourself to this?" I growled at him the moment Gift was out of hearing. "Why do you live to make my life miserable?"

"I didn't invite myself." He countered.

"You could have said no?"

"Why? So, you can feel better?" He demanded.

I took a swing at him, but he merely caught my wrist and held on tightly.

"You've had your shot." Storm told me angrily. "Try that again, and I *will* make you suffer."

"Let go. You're hurting me."

He released me but shoved my hand away, forcing me to stagger backward.

He walked up to the beautiful glass door and pulled it open. By the time I reached it, it was already closing again, causing me to crash face-first into the glass. I was sure he heard the sound, but he didn't so much as look back.

We got the table, thankfully.

The moment we sat, our table was swarmed with girls. I arched a brow but realized they were all talking at Storm.

"I love your band!" One of then squealed happily. "Can I take a picture with you?"

"Um—I'm kind of out with friends right now." He told her.

She looked crestfallen but nodded. The other girls seemed to get the picture and they hung their heads and walked away.

I could still see a few of them snaping pictures of Storm.

I chewed on the inside of my lips.

"What was that about, P?" Gift wanted to know.

"I'm a music major." He explained. "My band *Base Note* has a little bit of a following."

"You play in a band!" She squealed like a fan girl. "How did I not know this? Who's in it?"

"Myself, Seua, Kai." He replied.

"What about the other cutie?" Gift asked.

"Gear?" He smiled. "No—he is more of a behind the scenes kind of guy. He makes us look good."

Dinner was torture.

Aside from people who kept coming to our table to speak with Storm, forcing us to move to a private area, it was like Gift and Storm were on a date and I was the third wheel.

Storm spent the entire time in deep conversation with Gift. When I cared enough to eaves drop, they were talking about guitars and foreign coffee. They were discussing international landmarks and designer cars—I knew nothing about any of those things.

I'd never had fancy coffee or driven in a fancy car.

Yes, I was definitely the third wheel.

He laughed with her, created inside jokes with her, touched her arm as they talked.

At one point, she was putting food onto his plate and that was when I jerked from the table, paused to tell them I was going to the bathroom but stopped myself. Instead of speaking, I left for the toilet.

I doubt either of them would notice I was gone.

After using the facilities, and was standing by the sink, I couldn't help staring at myself in the mirror. For a moment, I closed my eyes and allowed my mind to wander. It immediately went to Storm—the darkness of his hair that always looked as if he was tossing in bed. The stark brown of his eyes, the plumpness of his lips—if I let myself admit it, Storm was handsome.

I wanted to know if he smelled like temptation and fire—the kind of temptation I would gladly fall into, the kind of fire I wanted to be consumed by.

As I remained there, I closed my eyes and allowed my head to fall backward. I wondered what his kiss tasted like.

Gasping, I allowed my eyes to snap open, and I looked down at the front of my pants to see that I was aroused.

"No!" I screeched.

What's happening?

I didn't want those thoughts about Storm.

34

I didn't want to be curious about any of the carnal things my mind and body wanted.

I couldn't understand the feelings creeping through my veins, that had dug under my skin and rooted themselves there. I couldn't understand why seeing them together the way they were bothered me so much.

He spoke to her with kindness, laughed with her, ate food she placed on his plate—

Frustrated, I caught cold water in my hands and splashed my face.

When I went back to the table, the two of them were still talking as if I hadn't left.

Neither of them looked up to ask if I was okay. Still, I sat again and ate a little.

The two of them were still there as if they were longtime friends and I knew if I stayed, I'd say something or do something.

The green-eyed monster in me would break free and then I'd have to deal with the fallout from that.

"Um—" I pulled money from my wallet and placed it by my plate then gathered my bag.

"I'm not feeling well." I cleared my throat. "I'm going to head back."

"We came together." Gift protested, trying to hand me back my money. "Let me take care of the bills and we can go."

"Yeah. You guys are having fun." I refused to accept the money back. "I just want to go home and lay down."

"Come on, Wind." Gift pleaded. "A little longer."

"I don't feel well, P." I stressed my point by sliding out from the table, pushed my chair in and walked out of the restaurant.

Outside, I doubled over, trying to catch my breath for a second before walking north back toward the dorms.

When I realized it was a bit of a walk, I got on a bus that let me off around the corner then walked the rest of the way.

I showered, changed into my pajamas then sat at my desk to do a final review for my test the next day. I also stole a few minutes to print off a few monologues for my audition.

I was almost finished when my mother called, and I tried as best I could to keep my anxiety out of my voice.

"You didn't tell me about your roommate." Mae curled herself into my father's old chair and lifted a mug of tea to her lips. "Is he from a good family?"

"I don't know much about his family."

"Do you at least get along?"

"I'm not sure." I told her. "We don't spend much time together. He's my senior and has his own friends. It's a little weird trying to hang out with them."

"Well, I should talk to him. Ask him to take care of you."

"Mae, I can take care of myself." I stressed. "I don't need a strange guy looking out for me."

"He shouldn't still be a strange guy, should he?" She sipped. "You've been at school a few weeks now."

"It's just—I can handle this." I assured her. "If I need help, I'll ask P'Gift. I don't want to bother my roommate and be a burden."

I quickly changed the subject to my test the next day and told her how anxious I was because of it.

"I'm sure, you'll do fine." My mother encouraged. "My son is very smart."

"Thanks, Mae." I laughed softly. "How are you doing? You're not overworking, are you? I worry about you."

"It's not your job to worry about me." She reminded me.

"You're my mother. You're all I have." I admitted freely. "I can't lose you."

Mae blew me kisses over video chat causing me to smile. "I wish your father was here to see you. He would have been so proud."

"Mae." I blushed.

"I'm serious." Mae promised. "I never had the chance to go to university. And he had to drop out halfway in because his family ran out of money. All he ever wanted for you was better than we had. Your father loved me more than words—I knew that. But you, Sunan Rattanaksin, you were the love of his life."

I blushed.

My father doted on me. It wasn't to say he didn't ensure I was respectable and a halfway decent person. He was very strict when it came to certain things.

But I never had to wonder if there was love there.

"When they placed you in his arms as a tiny baby, he fell in love right away." She admitted. "He fell right into father role immediately. When it came time for you to go down for sleep, he wouldn't let you go—he cuddled you on his chest. We had to wait until he fell asleep then took you to your bassinet."

"I miss him, Mae."

"I know you do, my love." A tear toppled down her cheek. "I miss him too. Did you know your father was the only man I'd ever been with?"

"Really?"

She nodded. "I saw him for the first time when I was fourteen. He probably didn't even know I existed because he was already twenty. But I knew he was the man I would marry. Then he went away for ten years—when I saw him again—I had to make my move."

My cheeks flushed. "Mae!"

"If I didn't, you wouldn't be here."

"I'm still shy hearing my mother speak like this."

She giggled. "You are old enough now to understand how love works, Wind."

I nodded.

We talked for a little longer before she yawned.

"Go to sleep, Mae."

"I will, my love." She waved at me.

"I love you."

"I love you too, Sunan."

I allowed her to hang up first before closing my laptop and sat on my bed.

After plugging in my phone to charge, I attached my headphones and sat in the center of my bed, digging through my musical app to find Storm's band.

"What did he say his band was called?" I frowned until I remembered and typed in *Base Note.*

There were seven songs that seemed to be from their only album called *Circles.* I read the biography and it seemed Storm was their lead singer and guitarist.

I didn't know he could sing.

I pressed play on the first song, prepared to laugh out loud. Storm didn't seem like the singer type—I didn't feel he had the soul of a real musician.

But as his voice filled my head, I had no choice but to melt at the smooth perfection of it—his tone.

No wonder those girls were falling all over him. His looks, with this voice and the image of him on that guitar—it made sense.

I listened while trying to pick between the monologues I'd printed from the websites P'Seua had suggested.

But I was more caught up in the music I was listening to, than focusing on monologues. How could I not be taken in by his voice?

By the end of the mini-album, I had a favourite song I probably should never admit to—*Take My Body.*

The lyrics were sexy and though they made me blush, it spoke about the kind of relationship I dreamed of having with a lover one day.

Though I wanted to listen to the album for a second time, I didn't. Instead, I began playing English music. I needed to distract my brain from the soul in Storm's voice.

In the middle of rocking out to my music and refocusing on the monologues, Storm returned.

I didn't so much as look up to acknowledge his presence. He yanked my headphones off and dropped them on the bed beside me.

"Don't ignore me when I'm talking to you!" He told me crossly.

"If you don't like it, move out." I countered.

When he stepped back to rest his hands on his hips to glare at me, I put my phones back on and turned up the music.

Storm

After band practice, I stopped at the dorm to grab my gym bag. Wind wasn't there and I assumed he was out with his girlfriend again.

Forcing myself not to think about it, I checked my bag to make sure I had everything, then headed to the gym.

When I walked in, Kai was already there warming up.

"I know I'm late." I called as I rushed by Kai. "Give me two minutes."

Quickly, I changed, shoved my bag into the locker and slammed it shut. When I rushed out into the gym to where Kai was, I had him help me tape my hands for the gloves then we began sparring.

It didn't take long for either of us to realize my mind wasn't into it.

It wasn't like I could hide anything from him. Kai had known me most of my life.

After about forty-five minutes, Kai grabbed a couple bottles of water and we sat on the floor together.

"Tell me this," Kai said after a long drink from his bottle. "Is it really worth all of this trouble?"

"What?"

"You know what." A frown creased his handsome face. "I'm sure I don't have to go into details."

"You know it is." I replied in frustration. "It's just a little frustrating right now, but I can do this."

I loved Muay Thai and the fact that I had dropped the ball made me ashamed.

"Storm, if you were still competing, I couldn't let you go into the ring in this state of mind." Kai pointed out.

"I wasn't that bad—was I?"

"You're not focused—at all. When was the last time you got a full night's sleep? Uninterrupted except for bathroom breaks?"

I dragged my hand over my head.

"That's what I'm talking about." Kai frowned. "You're not sleeping. You're barely eating. You have the band. You have the—"

"I can do this." I told him. "I have to do this. If I don't, I'll never sleep again."

"Now, you're being dramatic."

"Trust me on this." I sighed and lifted the bottle to my lips again. "I'm heading home tomorrow for the weekend. I should be able to get some rest then. Good?"

Kai wrinkled his brows the way he always did when he was about to call me out on my bullshit.

Instead, his muscular shoulders rose and fell heavily.

"Fine. But if I have to call Papa and make him force you to rest, I'll do it."

I chuckled. "I'll rest—the only thing I'll do while there is cook, do a little fiddling with some music and homework. All if it will be done from the pool deck or bed."

"Right." Kai shook his head, but he was smiling.

"I'll be okay. You'll see."

We finished up and left to head home in our own vehicles.

I was soaked from a downpour running across the parking lot to the entrance and by the time I made it to my room, lightning was streaking across the sky, lighting up the space.

I turned on the lamp by my bed, then rushed across to the window to pull the curtains in place.

As thunder scraped across the sky, Wind groaned in his sleep.

I shifted to look at him—his brows were knitted as he thrashed about on the bed.

"Pa." He cried. "Don't leave me. Please, don't leave me."

The pain in his voice threatened to bring me down.

"Wait for me." Wind pleaded.

Tears filtered through his lashes and rolled down the side of his head as he begged his father to stay, to wait.

I rushed to change into dry clothes, dragged a towel over my hair to stop the strands from dripping then went back and knelt beside his bed.

Tenderly, I pressed my palm to his cheek. It was only meant to tame whatever demons he had chasing him inside his head. He simply snuggled his cheek into my palm and went back to sleep.

"It's okay." I whispered using my free hand to move his hair off his forehead, wishing I could place a kiss there. "I know I'm nothing like your father. But I'm here and I'm not leaving you."

When I lifted my hands away to sit on the floor beside his bed, he grimaced, whimpered and whispered for his father.

Sad, I massaged the wrinkles from the center of his forehead.

Not wanting to leave him, I allowed him to hold my hand all night as the thunder bellowed around us. It was so loud, it felt almost as if it was shaking the foundation of the building around us.

Before he woke the next morning, I gently took my hand away from him, pulled the sheets up to his shoulders and reluctantly walked away.

I took a quick shower, dressed then grabbed my things and left the room, walking away trembling.

Standing beside his bed, listening to his anguished cries, feeling the tightness the way he squeezed my hand—staying the night with him left me broken.

I knew if I stayed at school all day I wouldn't survive. Instead, I went to my morning class, then hit the road home to my grandfather's place.

That gated mansion had always been a sanctuary for me. Having my grandfather there always calmed me in a way that was almost otherworldly.

Even at my age, I still felt peace and love there.

When I arrived, I parked my Bentley beside my grandfather's convertible and entered the house.

I knew precisely where to find him—his library with his numerous books.

Dropping my bag at the door, I entered, fell to my knees beside him and rested my head in his lap.

He put his book aside and caressed my hair back from my face. "Storm?"

I couldn't speak.

"Klahan?"

Still, the words I wanted to give him didn't even reach my throat.

"What's the matter?" He pushed softly.

"Please, Papa. Just let me sit here for a moment."

"Okay." He nodded. "Take as much time as you need."

I wasn't sure how long I was in that moment before I lifted my head and pulled myself off the floor to hug him.

"*Sawatdii khrap,* Papa."

"Why don't I get you something to eat," Papa said. "You take a shower and get some rest. You can tell me what's happening tomorrow."

"*Khob Khun,* Papa."

Leaving him, I showered and when I descended the stairs again, he had food ready for us to eat. We ate in silence, but I could feel his eyes on me.

His curiosity burned a hole in my head, and I couldn't help but meet his eyes.

"He accepted the scholarship." I admitted to Papa. "He is my roommate. But he hates me."

"He doesn't hate you—he hates what you did. There is a difference."

"Trust me, Papa. He told me he hated me." I admitted. "And the look in his eyes—I mean, we say things we don't mean all the time. But his eyes weren't lying."

43

"This is affecting you badly." Papa reached over to hold one of my hands. "Maybe you should just call it quits and move to your father's condo close to the campus."

"I can't." I pulled my hand away to pick up my drink. "I've waited so long."

"Sometimes all you can do is just let go and wait."

"I'm going to call Gear." I slipped from the stool and picked up my late. "I didn't tell him I was coming home. Thank you for dinner, na?"

Papa smiled.

I could see he wanted to talk more, but I was exhausted and wasn't sure how much more my brain could handle. I scraped the rest of my dinner into the garbage, placed my plate into the dishwasher and left the room for my bedroom.

After closing the door, I plugged my phone in to charge, then knelt in front of my bed to pull out a box I'd bought when I was seventeen to keep private things in. Slowly, I lifted the lid and pulled out the sealed letter that sat on the top. The edges were creased to melting away since it had been handled so many time.

"*Kho tod māk.*" I whispered. "*P kho tod.*"

I fell asleep on the floor and woke up that way the next morning in pain.

The hard floor was hell on my back, neck and ribs.

I dropped the letter back into the box, closed it and shoved it under my bed.

Instead of climbing into bed, I changed and went for a run, hoping it would work out the soreness in me. I hoped the fresh air would make me feel better.

When I returned, Papa was trying to move down the stairs, but his knees seemed to be acting up again. I rushed forward and helped him down and he patted my head like he usually did when I was a kid.

I smiled.

A quick shower later, I joined Papa to make breakfast and after we ate, I stocked the dishwasher and started it.

He went to his books, and I grabbed my phone and sat on the pool deck with my feet in the water to call Gear.

"You didn't tell me you were going home to Papa." Gear frowned. "I wanted to go home too."

"I'm sorry." I told him. "I needed some Papa time."

"Are you okay?"

"I am now." I offered him a smile. "Don't worry—I'm with Papa. I'm fed, safe and resting."

"I'm worried about you." Gear admitted. "You haven't been the same since you moved into the dorms. It dawned on me that P'Wind is the guy you were looking for, right?"

I nodded.

"Then why aren't you happier?" Gear asked.

"Because I caused him pain." I admitted out loud for the first time. "I hurt him and it's the kind of hurt he probably will never forgive me for."

"I don't understand." Gear shook his head. "If he'll never forgive you, how can you expect this plan of yours to work?"

"It won't."

"But P, that's going to break your heart." Gear pointed out.

My heart was already hurting even as I nodded. "I'll be okay."

Gear pressed his lips into a thin line. "I hate leaving you like this, but I'm already late."

"Late—for what?"

"The auditions for the film are coming up, remember?" Gear reminded me. "I have to meet with P'Seua to talk to him about what he wants with the pictures, that sort of thing. I've been meaning to ask you, are you writing the theme song for the film?"

I shrugged. "I don't know. Seua is going to be using the new song I've written, but he hasn't asked if I wanted to write the theme song."

"Well, who else is he going to ask?"

I chuckled. "Go to your meeting."

"Are you going to be okay?" Gear was already moving around the room to get his camera and a bag. "I can talk to you on my way there. P'Kai is picking me up."

"What happened to your car?"

"Nothing—why?" He arched a brow.

"You seem to be spending a lot of time with, *P'Kai* lately." I smirked.

Gear rolled his eyes. "Are you going to be okay?"

"Okay, *khrap*." I even had the energy to give him a thumbs up.

Gear smiled and was gone.

Exhaling, I set the phone beside me and stretched out on my back to stare up at the clear, blue sky. For a while, I simply looked up but at some point, I fell asleep.

I hate you.

Wind's voice haunted my dreams.

Each time I tried going back to sleep on the deck, the words dug into my brain, flowed through my veins and pulsed off my heart and my very soul. Eventually, I gave up, ensured I had nothing in my pockets and jumped into the pool.

Papa loved it when I sang for him. He especially loved my original songs. After dinner and the cleanup, I sat with him on the balcony outside his bedroom and played *Remember Fireflies* for him.

At the end of the song, Papa nodded for a silent moment then sniffled.

"Wow." He smiled. "Your grandmother would have loved this song."

"Really?"

He nodded. "I don't think I've ever told you the story of how I met her."

"No." I leaned forward after setting my guitar on the floor by my leg. "Tell me."

"She fell in love with me long before I knew who she was." He admitted. "Apparently, she saw me out with some friends and thought I was out of her league. She was a waitress at this bar I frequented with my friends. She would go in on the night she knew I'd be there. After a while, she fell in love but thought I was out of her league."

"Oh. Did she give up?"

"Almost." Papa admitted. "She thought all she could do was love me from a distant, that there would never be a day when I would look at her as anything but a waitress in a bar. It weighed on her."

"But you got married and had a child."

"We got married and had a child." Papa grinned proudly.

"There's a story there."

Papa nodded. "Of course, there is."

"Well?" I asked.

"Well, what?" He smirked.

"Tell me!"

"One night one of my friends got a little more drunk than usual. He wasn't taking no for an answer, and I stepped in. She was so beautiful. That was the night, she was done. She was going to move on because she thought it was never going to happen."

"She would have loved *Remember Fireflies*."

Papa nodded. "You're so talented, Storm. This is why I went to bat for you with your father."

"I won't let you down, Papa. I promise."

Though I spent time with Papa, I also hid away in my room, doing homework and working on the second song for *Base Note*.

By the end of the first day, I had a rough song ready and sent it to Seua and Kai to see what they thought, then continued playing about with the guitar, creating new music without lyrics.

From time to time, I was tempted to call Wind, to hear his voice, to see how he was doing.

But I knew that would do me no good.

Wind wouldn't want to talk to me. Shaking my head, I set my guitar in the holder by my bed and walking over to the glass doors leading to the balcony.

Night had descended and I could hear the crickets singing in the dark. I closed my eyes, shivered at the cool air floating up off the ocean, and smelling the faint smell of what remained of the sea air.

I remembered the day Wind stormed into the house I was raised in. I wasn't at all sure how he managed to get by the men at the gate—I didn't get a chance to ask. I was laughing at first—thinking he was just some kid who needed a little money for whatever wrong I'd done to him. My mother, before she left, always taught me that money could solve everything.

But Wind had taken the money and whipped it back at my head. The bills rained down over me, one slicing my cheek as it dragged over my flesh to the floor.

"This is your happiness." Wind explained, inching closer and closer to me until every time he breathed, his chest brushed mine. "Not mine. You have some nerve."

"How about a little respect?"

"I'll give you the same respect I give a bug before I squash it under my boot." The rage in his tear-filled eyes terrified me. He gave off an aura that should have had me trembling.

Still, I faced him, stood toe to toe with him and braced myself for whatever he had to throw at me.

He hadn't hit me—his words alone tore me to shreds and left me bloodied and extremely tiny. He cursed me—wished nothing but hell for my life.

"I hope one day you will feel the pain I'm feeling." Wind told me, his face so close to mine, his heated breath washed over my face.

I remembered he smelled like cinnamon.

"What do you want?" I had demanded. "You don't want money—what else is there?"

"Your pain." Wind replied harshly.

I scoffed.

"I want you to feel it, so you know what it's like to have your heart ripped from your chest." He continued through gritted teeth. "To lose everything. Then you'll know why I'll never, *never* forgive you."

His lips trembled and I knew he was fighting to keep from crying. I tried speaking but he merely backed up and left the same way he'd entered, like a force of nature.

I lowered my head.

Wind was getting his wish.

It hurt seeing him with Gift, watching the way he smiled at everyone else but me. It tore my heart to shreds knowing he liked her, that he was with her, touching her—*being* with her.

I wanted to give up.

The pain that vibrated through me made me want to stop, to walk away, to hide. Gritting my teeth, I bowed my head so low, I rested my head on the rail.

But even as I hurt, I knew I couldn't give in.

"Storm?" Papa called, followed by a knock.

"On the balcony, Papa."

I stood, straightened my spine, and turned to face Papa. I didn't want to show him how low I had fallen. Though he knew I ran home because the world and Wind hadn't been kind, I didn't want him to see just how far I'd fallen because of this.

He hadn't wanted me to get involved with Wind again. He'd had to pick me up off the floor when I came to my senses and realized what I'd caused to happen.

My father had no sympathy. He didn't even come home.

My mother was an entirely other sort of cruel I hadn't seen coming.

When Papa shuffled through the door, I couldn't help the way my heart filled. He looked like my father, only his hair had gone completely white.

He leaned heavily on his cane, an injury he suffered three years before in a car accident. Sometimes it was worse than other times, but I was grateful he was alive and with me.

Papa stood beside me, and I turned to look out over the view. For an eternity, neither of us said anything.

"I'm tired, Papa." I admitted.

I wouldn't tell that to Kai or Gear. It was something that had been sitting on my chest ever since the day Wind barged into my house.

"Do you want to give up?" He asked. "There is no shame in saying, I can't do this."

"I can't give up." I told him. "Because if I do, one day he'll find out that I gave up, that I gave up on him."

"Then take these few days here with me, breathe through, rest and then try again." He patted my back. "There's no shame in saying you need a break, that you feel battered and bruised and that you need a moment."

"Then I need a moment."

Papa nodded and pulled me into his arms. I snuggled my face into his neck and sighed. Papa rubbed my back until I regained my strength. When I stepped away, all I could do was smile at him.

"Thanks, Papa."

"Boy." He chortled. "You know I have nothing but time for you and your brother. This has always been your safe space—for as long as you need it."

"I'll always need it."

Papa ruffled my hair and I smiled.

Wind

The night before was a Thursday—that meant the Friday Storm had classes. I expected him to be home at least early Friday morning in order to get ready for classes. When he didn't show up Friday, I took the time to make myself breakfast in the kitchen neither of us had used since moving in and sat on the floor between our beds to eat. The tiny table at the corner was uncomfortable and the chair dug into my thighs when I used it before.

I started my day in peace and quiet, not anxiety that he and I would get into it again. I'd tried getting the school to switch me to another dorm the first week I had been there, but apparently, they were fully booked.

After dressing, I packed, ensuring I had my homework and wallet, then left the dorm, even whistling as I went. There was something airy floating through me that made it almost like I could be walking on a cloud. I got through the first half of my day, then stopped in the canteen to eat. A few of my classmates stopped by to ask me some questions about what I thought of our test the day before then left me alone to my silence.

By the time I finished my classes for the day and met up with Gift to practice my audition piece, I wasn't as exhausted as I normally was by this time in the day. Stopping at the small diner close to campus, I bought myself a passionfruit slushie then hurried to the Dramatic Arts building where I'd book a practice room for us.

"You look happy." Gift was busy pulling her shoes off at the door when I met up with her.

"Mmm."

"Did you murder P'Storm and hide his body in the room?"

I winced and toed off my shoes. "I did no such thing. He didn't come home last night. I had the room all to myself."

"Good—where is he?"

"I don't know." I offered her a shrug while slurping from my drink. "Why should I care?"

"Your roommate didn't tell you he was leaving. And he didn't come home like he should have and you're not worried?"

"I'm not his father." I walked by her and headed down the small aisle between the seats. "He doesn't have to report to me where he's going or what he's doing."

"That's not the point."

"Then what is your point?"

"I don't know why you're not taking this more seriously." Gift followed. "Has he ever gone away overnight and not said anything? We live in dangerous times, you know?"

"Don't be paranoid, P." I told her. "He's probably at his brother's or P'Kai or even P'Seua."

She pulled out her phone and I watched as she tapped away at it.

When she put it away, I sighed and set my drink down to find the monologue I'd chosen and handed it over to her.

She'd just accepted it when her phone went off.

Gift read the screen then turned it so I could read the screen.

Gift: is P'Storm with you?

P'Seua: No.

P'Kai: No and he's not with Gear either.

"Any questions?" Gift asked.

My heart sank.

"See?" She asked.

"Then where is he?" I muttered.

"That's my question to you." Gift took a slurp from my drink. "Anyway, let's see what you have."

I got through practice and after leaving Gift, I decided to walk back to the dorm. I tapped my foot impatiently as the elevator made its slow way up through the shaft. I squeezed through the doors before they were open wide enough and ran all the way to our door. Pausing a moment to catch my breath, I let myself in, but the space was empty.

When I knocked on the bathroom, no one answered. I opened the door and poked my head in—Storm wasn't there.

"Oh, this is bad." I muttered, resting my hand on my hips and turning to look around.

His bed was made. His section was neat and tidy. He hadn't been into the dorm all day. So, he slept somewhere else the night before and was still not home.

I waited—darkness grew thick and silent around the building and my worries mounted. At some point, I fell asleep but woke with a start in the early hours of the morning.

A check of his bed told me he still hadn't returned.

What if Gift had been right and I should have been worried before? What if he was dying in a ditch somewhere? What if he was lost and couldn't find his way back?

I spent the rest of the night, tossing and turning with every doomsday scenario flashing through my mind. The next morning, I snuck over to his Muay Thai gym, but he wasn't there.

I wandered to the usual places I suspected a man like him would go—the canteen, the music building, the diner—but he wasn't at any of them.

Since I didn't have contact with any of his friends, or had his number, I had no way of digging further. To make matters worse, I was too much of a coward to talk to his friends or approach his brother. I secretly followed them around to see if he would join them.

He didn't.

Exhausted, I made my way back to my dorm and was broken hearted to not find him there, sitting on his bed, strumming away at his guitar.

Storm was gone the entire weekend and by Sunday I was a nervous wreck. I was finally planning to swallow my fear and reach out to Seua, Gear and Kai late Sunday night when I heard keys in the door. I quickly turned off my light and rolled over to face the wall, pretending I was asleep.

My worry immediately disappeared and was replaced with anger I never thought I was capable of anymore. How dare he leave and stay gone for so long without notice?

Was he with a girl?

Was she pretty?

I closed my eyes and force myself to calm down and that helped me to fall asleep.

The next morning, I woke up a little earlier than normal. I didn't want to face him because if I did, I knew I would say something I'd later regret.

But Storm was awake and in the shower ahead of me.

I banged on the door.

"You don't even have classes early!" I yelled. "Get out!"

"Occupied!" He replied.

"And where the hell have you been?"

He opened the door and leaned in close to meet my eyes.

"Patpong." He growled.

That word stopped me in my tracks and broke my heart.

Agitated, I dressed, grabbed my bag and left.

I definitely couldn't have faced him then. That one word had me more frazzled than I'd cared to admit, and I didn't want him to know he'd caused me such emotional turmoil.

The day dragged by, slowly—almost at a snail's pace. I stopped at the canteen to get myself something to wake me up. I leaned forward to peer into the case.

"Are you trying to wake up, or calm down?" The male voice asked from behind me.

I straightened my body and turned to smile at him. He was taller than I was, hair a deep blue and styled perfectly away from his face. This student was good-looking but wasn't Storm-good-looking.

I sighed but smiled at him.

"To wake up, P." I replied. "It's been a rough weekend."

"Partied too much?"

"I wish." I admitted around a chuckle.

"You're Wind."

I arched a brow. "Yes, P."

"I'm in your English class." He smiled. "Bank. And you don't have to call me P. I'm pretty sure I'm supposed to call you that."

I flushed. "How so?"

"You are a year late in, right?" He asked. "The class is fascinated by you. You're the one who won the first ever full ride scholarship to this school. No one has ever managed to score as high as you."

"So, what do you suggest to wake up?"

Bank stepped by me and called an order to the woman behind the counter. It took a couple of minutes before she came back with a drink that was brown with whipped cream on top. I took a sip and was delighted.

"Thank you." I pulled money out to pay, but Bank declined.

"My treat," he said. "One day I will ask you to tutor me. English is not my strongest subject."

I laughed. "I'm not perfect, you know."

"No one is." Bank paused to make his order. "But you're smart. I know you are."

As we walked away from the counter, I stopped to face him. "How did you know about my scholarship?"

Bank laughed. "Are you kidding? You're all over the Brainy Hottie Facebook page."

"I'm sorry—what?"

Bank drew something up on his phone and handed it over. The page was about students the females thought were hot who were also very smart. The fact I was on it seemed weird since I never thought I was good looking.

It seemed someone had followed me around and had taken pictures of me without my knowledge.

I looked around but everyone was going on about their business.

No one was paying me any attention. I handed his phone back.

"I'm not cute." I told Bank.

"Not according to all these girls." He smirked.

Shaking my head, I took a drink from my straw. "I have to go practice."

"Practice?"

I nodded. "I'm auditioning for the student film the club is making."

"Nice! I heard about it, but I can't act to save my life." Bank teased.

"Bank, I'm going out on a limb here…"

Bank arched a brow at me. "About what?"

"Would you like to exchange LINE?"

He grinned, and handed me his phone and I added my LINE ID and handed it back. He quickly sent me a message so I could have his and I left him to rush to my next class. I waited for the elevator and the moment I stepped in, someone called for me to hold the doors.

Without thinking, I did so while looking down at my phone to a message my mother had sent me.

When the person was close, I stepped back to allow them in and replied to my mother. I put the phone away just as the door slid shut and looked up to see the person who'd entered was Storm.

My heart immediately began racing, my cheeks flushed, and I shimmied to the far side of the tight space. Though he said nothing to me, I could feel his eyes on me, warming my body as if slowly catching me on fire.

My mind quickly switched gears when a loud screech filled the air and the elevator jerked. I knew it'd stopped moving—I could feel it.

I also knew we were stuck.

Correction—I was stuck.

In an elevator.

With Storm.

A warm swirl filled the pit of my stomach. My lungs couldn't take enough air fast enough as I jammed my finger into the emergency call button.

"You can stop now." Storm told me. "The light is flashing and that means they've received the call."

"Don't talk to me." I panted, still jamming my finger into the button.

He caught my hand and tugged it away and I retaliated by shoving him into the hard side of the elevator. Storm winced but only reached out and yanked me away from the button.

"Stop it!" He growled. "Sit!"

When I disobeyed, he shoved me to my ass on the floor. I merely curled into myself as panic filled me, making me dizzy.

"It wasn't my fault." He told me.

"Is something wrong with your hearing?" I demanded.

A voice came from the small speaker. It assured us they were working on getting the elevator unstuck.

Storm sat on the floor beside me and brought his knees up to wrap his arms around them.

"I know it doesn't seem like it," he said. "But I'm trying to do right. It may seem like it's too late, but I don't think it is. It's never too late to do the right thing."

For a moment, I turned to stare at him, to see the way his jawlines were set, and to admire the flawlessness of his face.

My phone rang.

"Gift?" I picked it up. "I'm stuck in the elevator."

"Your luck is horrible." She teased. "I'm waiting outside. There are men here trying to get you out, so don't worry. Are you alone?"

"No."

"Who's with you?"

"You'd never guess." I told her.

"P'Storm? Oh my."

I sighed. "Tell them to hurry? I feel like my chest is about to explode."

Gift promised she would, told me to remain calm and hung up.

But we were in the elevator a while. I'd abandoned my drink in a corner and my entire body was now shaking. Storm must have seen that something was wrong for he shifted close to me, took both my hands in his and began rubbing them.

"You have to calm down." He cooed. "Deep, slow breaths."

I was still angry at him, but his eyes were so beautiful, so reassuring. The softness of his voice calmed me, set my heart racing for an entirely different reason. Suddenly, I was okay but tired, so tired, I could barely keep my eyes open.

He let me rest my head on his shoulder and I sighed helplessly and closed my eyes.

When I woke again, the space around me was different. The familiar sterile scent of a hospital filled my nose and I groaned.

"Wind?" Gift called. "Are you okay?"

I tried sitting up, but she merely eased me back into the pillow. "Where am I?"

"Hospital." She replied. "I was worried. You passed out in the elevator. I wanted to take you home, but Storm insisted on having you be checked out by a doctor."

"P'Storm?"

"He's fine."

"Are you sure?" I pushed while sitting up.

"Wind, I'm sure." She promised. "Calm down. We don't need you freaking out right now, understand? Storm is a big boy. He can take care of himself."

I wanted to ask where he was, to demand to see him for myself before I could calm down, but Gift would have questions I didn't have answers for. Thinking he was in danger worried me.

My phone chimed, and Gift brought it over to me. It was a message from Bank asking if I was okay.

"*Yes.*" I responded. "*Why?*"

Instead of words, he sent me a picture.

It was Storm, carrying me as I curled into his chest. From the looks of it, he was carrying his lover. My cheeks burst into flames as I wanted to cry.

The second picture was of Storm kneeling by my side, holding my hand while the paramedics worked on me.

The third picture had him pressing a kiss to my forehead and I squeezed my eyes closed, wanting to feel what that was like to have his lips against my skin.

"It's a cute picture." Gift stared at my phone.

"Was he worried?" I asked.

She didn't answer my question. Instead, she walked over to where someone had set up a table with glasses, a jug with water and some ice-cubes. She filled a glass, dumped a few cubes in and brought it over to me.

"*I'm on my way.*" Bank sent me another text.

"*You don't have to.*" I sent him.

But he didn't reply.

"Who's Bank?" Gift asked.

"He's in my English class." I sighed, tired. "He's sweet."

Gift giggled.

"No." I told her. "I can't focus on anything like that right now."

Bank showed up and Gift left us alone. He arrived with a small teddy bear which made me laugh.

"It was short notice." He set the toy beside me on the bed then pulled up a chair. "What happened?"

"Elevator malfunction, I'm thinking. But I have to get out of here soon." I told him. "I have an audition—what time is it?"

"Just after five."

"I have an audition at seven that I can't miss." I shifted to push my legs out of the bed.

"Maybe we should talk to a doctor first." Bank told me. "Let me find one."

He ran from the room and returned with a doctor who checked me out and gave me the go-ahead to leave.

I was gathering my things when Storm stepped through the door and glared at Bank who was in the process of helping me pushed my arm into my jacket.

"I can do that." Storm told him.

"P'Storm…" I managed.

"I'll take you home." Storm told me.

I wanted to argue but knew it would be a useless waste of energy. Storm took my hand and led me from the room and down to his car where he opened the door for me.

"I have my audition tonight." I told him.

"You were in a hospital bed just a second ago." Storm pointed out.

"It's an audition, P'Storm." I told him. "It's not hard. And I refuse to let P'Seua down."

"Fine—you have some time. I'll drive you back."

Storm took me back the dorm, made me some soup and after I ate, he set my alarm and relegated me to a nap. I had to admit, it was nice to be taken care of. It felt good having him be concerned over me, making sure I was okay.

I wondered if this was the kind of friendship, I would have had with him had I given him a chance.

True to his word, Storm woke me up in time to have another bowl of warm soup and to take a shower, so I'd be ready for me audition.

As he drove, I practiced my lines. I wasn't feeling one hundred percent, but I said nothing to Storm.

Seua must have seen it, because he suggested allowing me to audition the next day. But I didn't want to hold things up because I was feeling a bit dizzy.

I gripped the rail as I climbed to the stage, walked to the center and loudly introduced myself.

I looked around the room but didn't see Storm. I figured after dropping me off, he'd taken off again and though I was disappointed, I inhaled and began my monologue.

When I was finished, the small group assembled applauded, and I smiled and exited the stage.

"You'll know in two days." Seua told me.

"Thank you, P." I replied. "I'm going to head back to my room. I'm not feeling very good."

"Why don't I have Kai walk with you?"

"No, thank you." I told him. "I'm not that sick. I'll be okay. The fresh air will do me well."

"Give me your phone." He extended a hand.

I wasn't sure why, but I handed him my phone. Seua added his phone number then gave it back.

"Call if anything." He told me.

I offered him way, promising I would.

After another small conversation, I exited the theatre and hurried along the empty hall toward the exit.

I was still wondering where Storm had gone to. I figured he left to give me space since I hadn't been very kind to him.

It was raining but I didn't care. I'd always loved walking in the rain to feel the drops against my skin, soaking through my hair and draining down my back. I always thought the caress of the cool water was as close as I'd get to having a lover's caress and every time I could, I stood in downpours.

But the moment I stepped out into the water and the first drops fell onto my head, my entire world went dark.

SusuKhaa

Storm

In the rain, I scooped Wind into my arms, and he curled into me. I carried him back to the dorms and placed him on my bed knowing he'd soak through the sheets.

Holding my breath, I removed Wind's clothes. He was in trouble of getting sick and I was weak and aroused.

I didn't mean to—but how could I avoid not feeling something at the perfection of his body?

Holding my breath, I used a towel to dry his body, thinking of everything else but the way I wanted to kiss the water droplets from his body.

I pulled one of my sheets over him and was able to exhale again. I patted my cheeks to refocus on what I had to do and forced my feet to move across the room to Wind's closet. Hunching down, I dug through the closet, trying to find something to put on him. It had to be something that was easy to be worn, something that didn't require much lifting.

Settling on a pair of shorts and a graphic shirt, I dressed him then carried him to his bed and set him in the middle. His forehead was warm, a little warmer than it should be. I gathered a wet towel and pressed it to his skin.

Leaving him for a bit, I closed myself in the bathroom to splash cold water on my face.

I needed something to stop the racing of my heart, the burning of my body, the hardness between my legs.

The coldness was like a slap, but it didn't do much to soothe me.

After a few rounds of that, I dried my face and went back to Wind. I sat on the edge of his bed to stare down into his face.

"I know there was something here." I told him as he flinched in his sleep. "But it's clear to me now that I'm not your happiness. Gift is. And even though it kills me—your happiness is more important than anything I'm feeling or thinking."

I caressed his cheek then reached down to pull the sheets up to his shoulder. When I was walking away, Wind called out for his father.

The horror in his voice caused me to sit beside him again and framed his face with my palms. Every time he had a nightmare, wanting his father, it broke me.

"Don't be afraid, Wind." I spoke to him. "Don't be afraid."

After his father's death, I spoke to the people in the neighourhood about him. The man was a hero. Everyone loved him for he would give a person the very shirt off his back if they showed need. He was kind, funny loving—until he became sick. It seemed everyone rallied around him and his family, but it hadn't been enough.

Death had come calling and it wanted the father.

He held onto my hand, and I sat with him until he'd fallen into deep sleep. I left him long enough to ask Kai for a favour—buy some meds and porridge for the next morning. I spent the night going in and out of sleep, ensuring Wind was okay. At one point, I had to wipe him down with cold towels.

In the morning, Kai stopped by with porridge and the medication I needed for Wind, gave me a hug and left with the new song.

"P'Storm?"

I closed the door, walked through the galley kitchen to peer into the room. Wind was sitting up in bed, and all I wanted to do was crawl in with him and draw him into my arms. My heart fluttered as he'd never called me that before.

I smiled at him. "I'm here."

Wind swallowed and nodded.

When he fell back into the pillows, I went back into the kitchen to pour the porridge into a bowl then carried it and the pills back to sit beside him on the bed.

I tested his temperature by pressing a palm to his forehead. "Your fever is going away, but you're still a little warm. Here, drink this."

"Why are you doing this?" Wind asked.

"Because you needed the help." I replied.

"Is it because—"

"I didn't do it because I want you to like me." I interrupted. "I know you have no intentions of even contemplating that."

"P…"

"I did it because you were in trouble." I interrupted. "I did it because if Gear was in the position, I would want someone to step up and help him. No matter how much you hate me, helping is the right thing to do. Now, eat so you can regain your strength."

"Hate is a strong word."

"Like I said, past aside, you need to regain your strength." Turning, I removed one of the pills and extended it to him. "Take a swallow of the porridge and then this. You can call your girlfriend to take care of you now. I'll stay somewhere else tonight. She can use my bed if she wants—there are sheets in the closet."

Wind didn't argue.

I did as I suggested and while he ate, I packed a bag for the night.

Before leaving, I checked in on Wind but didn't leave until Gift knocked on the door. I let her in but said nothing.

I left, stopped at a supermarket to pick up some food then drove to Kai's condo.

My best friend said nothing.

He stepped aside to allow me in then closed the door. We left from his place to school and spent the day together with very few words passing between us.

We reported to band practice. After we finished working on our songs, we played a few tunes from Mew Suppasit.

I knew that was to cheer me up, but I didn't complain.

It made me feel much better than when I walked into the space.

I didn't go home that night—I didn't think I should. Instead, I lay beside Kai, while he slept, staring up at the darkened ceiling, my mind swirling like a tornado.

After a while, I couldn't seem to get comfortable no matter what side I was on.

Kai reached out and pressed a hand to my thigh closest to him. "Are you okay?"

"I can't sleep." I admitted. "Too much on my mind."

Kai groaned and sat up, reaching across to turn on the bedside lamp. He turned to curl my legs under himself to take my hand.

"Okay, talk to me." Kai told me.

"I'm just worried about Wind, that's all." I told him.

"Maybe you should call him."

I scoffed.

"Okay, answer me this." Kai leaned closer. "This thing with Wind, is it about what happened with his father or are you in love with him?"

"Love is a strong word."

"True." Kai nodded. "Better question—do you have feelings for Wind?"

"I think—I don't know." I admitted. "I've never been with a man before, but there's just something in the pit of my chest that—Kai, I can't make him happy, I can't fix any of this and it feels like I'm losing my life."

"It hurts because you care." Kai replied. "Caring always opens you up to pain."

"I guess." I bit into my bottom lip.

We tried sleeping again.

When that didn't work for me, I climbed out of bed, wandered into the living room, and called Gear.

"It's late, P'Storm." Gear moaned. "What's wrong?"

"I can't sleep."

"Have you tried warm milk?"

I sighed. "I shouldn't have called."

Gear tried stopping me, but I hung up and slumped backward into the sofa.

The one night I meant to stay away turned into two. Each time I thought to head back, I kept imagining walking in on Wind and Gift in a compromising position. Thankfully, when I did enter the room, Gift wasn't there, and neither was Wind.

I packed away my things, dumped dirty clothes into the laundry bag and plugged my phone in to charge. I changed my towel and entered the bathroom to shave and shower.

When I walked out again, I had a towel wrapped around my hips. Wind kind of froze when he saw me and at first, I wasn't sure what was happening.

I walked to my phone and checked to see if anyone had called or messaged.

The group chat with my friends had been busy, but before I could reply to any of the messages, heat roamed my body.

I blinked and looked to see that Wind had been undressing me with his eyes. His eyes roamed up my body then down again.

I had to admit, it felt good. The way he looked at me I hadn't had before. His eyes caused my breath to quicken, and I licked my lips. My nipples tightened under his gaze, and I stood there, waiting.

Waiting for what?

"This…" Wind managed.

"Wind?"

He gasped softly, looked away but only for a moment before his gaze returned to my framed and slowly lifted upward.

"Are you okay?" I asked him.

"Um—" Wind panted, grabbed his towel and locked himself into the bathroom.

I dressed and sat in front of my laptop to do some work. I refocused on the chatgroup, replying to the conversation I had missed while I cleaned myself.

Wind exited the bathroom, but I didn't look away from the message.

"Do you want to go out to dinner?" I asked Wind.

"Um—what?" Wind asked.

I looked up at Wind. "Dinner—do you want to go out for dinner?"

"I don't know if that's the best idea." Wind told me. "Do you?"

"How are we supposed to learn to get along if we don't spend time together?" I asked him. "What's the reason you're afraid to be alone with me?"

"I'm not afraid of being alone with you." Wind muttered irritated. "I live alone with you, don't I?"

"But you never want to be here with me unless we're both sleeping." I leaned closer to meet his eyes. "Are you attracted to me?"

"You're an idiot." Wind snapped.

I sighed. "It's just dinner. Gear, Kai and Seua will be there with us."

"Oh—okay. Sure."

I was still surprised when he agreed, but I didn't question it. Soon, we were in my car, driving to the restaurant. But when we got there, my friends didn't show up and Wind wanted to leave immediately.

"We're already here." I told him. "I'll kick their asses later, but let's just eat—my treat?"

"I don't want anything from you."

"Fine, then you can pay for your own dinner." I told him. "How long are you going to hate me?"

"For the rest of my life and yours." Wind admitted.

I sighed. "One dinner."

Wind gave in and we entered the space and was seated. But dinner wasn't fun. We had nothing to talk about and Wind spent the entire time on his phone. I assumed he was speaking to Gift. I gave up and called for the bill. I paid for both our meals then pushed from the table. We walked in silence out the door, but Wind stopped just as I stepped off the sidewalk.

"What's wrong?" I asked.

"Nothing." Wind replied. "I'm not going home with you. Thanks for dinner."

He was already walking away from me, heading in the opposite direction of where my car had been parked.

"Where are you going?" I asked.

"Don't wait up." He replied walking off.

Instead of going home, I followed Wind through the misting rain as he walked along the brightly lit streets.

He cut across a large parking lot, down a treelined path and through a park with lovers kissing around us. When he finally slowed, it was in front of a building where he waited until Gift came out. She quickly looped her arm with him as she leaned against her car with Wind standing in front of her.

She played with his shirt, unbuttoning the top one and giggling as they talked.

I wanted to throw up.

I wanted to scream, to rush across the space to force her to get her hands off him. But somehow, I found the courage to remain hidden, to watch what was happening even though it broke my heart.

When they climbed into Gift's car, I jammed my fingers into my pockets and returned to my car to drive home.

But I was stuck, frozen with my forehead against the steering, trying to make a few decisions. I realized then that I had to let go—that no matter how confused I was about my feelings for Wind, I had to let him go because he could never be mine.

Be mine?

I exhaled, feeling the heat of my breath gushing out my mouth, leaving me lightheaded.

To be safe, I stayed, parked in the same space, until I was feeling better.

By the time I arrived back at the dorm, all I wanted to do was curl myself in bed. I didn't even shower when I got there.

I barely changed into pajamas before I climbed under the sheets, turned my back toward the door and pulled the sheets up to my neck.

That night, I was awake when Wind returned.

I was awake as he showered then plugged his phone in and climbed into bed.

I was awake after he fell asleep, throughout the night and was awake when he climbed out of bed, showered and left for class.

Any words I wanted to give to him died in my throat and there was nothing else I could do. It took everything in me to even lift my head—but I was able to gather myself and gathered enough strength to attend classes.

Just before one class, I cornered Kai and Seua in a corridor and frowned.

"What do you think you were doing?" I demanded.

"We thought the two of you getting together could help you out." Seua explained. "How are the two of you supposed to work things out if you're barely in a room together long enough to say two words that don't end with one or both of you storming out?"

"That's not your concern!" I snapped. "I'm done—okay? I can't keep doing this because Wind have no intentions of changing his mind and it's not fair to him to put him in such a situation."

"You've fallen for him." Seua whispered.

"You don't know what you're talking about." I turned for the stairs.

Kai caught my arm and pull me back toward them. "It's a simple enough question."

"I don't know." I whispered fiercely.

70

Students rushed by us, and I paused to wait until we were alone again.

"I don't know." Bowing my head, I closed my eyes for a moment before meeting their eyes again. "He turns me on. It makes me happy to be around him but he's already in love. He already has a lover. I watch him with her, and I know being with me wouldn't make him happy."

"Storm." Seua whispered.

"Just stop, okay?" I pleaded. "Please."

Without saying another word, I turned and did climb the stairs away from them to face the rest of my day. Though I didn't want to face people anymore, I couldn't let Seua down and reluctantly reported to the film club.

"The music for the movie is in good hands." Seua beamed proudly. "*Base Note,* my band will handle that. Our very own P'Storm is writing our theme song."

I arched a brow. Though, he hadn't asked yet, but Gear was right, who else would he have asked.

"You didn't ask." I smiled.

"Did I have to?" Seua asked, blinking his eyelashes at me, causing the others in the room to laugh.

"You're lucky you're handsome." I teased.

"Does that mean you're in?" Seua asked.

I chuckled. "I'm in."

Seua fist-pumped. "Yes!"

After the introductions, Seua got around to the casting and all the potential cast members leaned forward as in unison.

"The leading couple." Seua spoke louder. "N'Wind and his lover will be played by P'Storm!"

The others cheered happily but my eyes were on Wind.

He blinked at Seua, then fainted.

Wind

It was hard to believe that Storm was kneeling over me. My arms were wrapped around him, his shirt opened as I kissed his warm abs then looked up into his stormy eyes.

I trembled, feeling weak, then as if I was floating on air and I didn't want it to end. I wanted him to keep looking at me like that until I was completely consumed with the power of his stare.

His palms were large against my shoulders, then down my back.

I wanted those hands on my bare flesh. I needed his lips on mine.

"Storm." I whispered. "Storm, please."

Arching forward, I tangled my arms tighter around him, needed to be closer—desperate to be a part of him.

Something fell against my left cheek then my right. The sound of a spark rippled through the air, and I forced my eyes opened.

At first, I wasn't sure where I was or what I should have been doing.

My head hurt.

"What happened?" I croaked.

Storm turned from his computer to stare at me blankly. He didn't speak and his silence made my head spin.

"What—"

"You fainted." Storm replied. "I'll give you a moment to remember why."

He returned his attention to what he'd been doing.

As I rubbed the back of my neck, memories of why I'd fainted slowly returned to me.

Angry, I shoved from the bed to spin Storm's chair so he could be looking at me while I yelled my frustrations at him.

"I don't get why every time I turn around, you're there." I frowned. "This was supposed to be something fun for me."

"This isn't about you."

"No?"

"I'm not having this argument with you, Wind."

Storm tried to turn his chair back to face his laptop, but I wouldn't let him.

He braced his palms to my chest and shoved until I toppled over. I hit the floor hard, but he didn't say anything—didn't apologize.

Though in pain, I couldn't focus on my back at the moment.

I wanted him dead.

When he swiveled his chair, I rose, angrier than ever and pushed the chair back so he had to face me.

"Why are you torturing me?" I demanded. "You couldn't have joined another club?"

"My being in the film club shouldn't have been a surprise to you." He replied. "That's number one. Number two, I've been a part of the film club since my first year here and I'm not about to quit because you can't learn to leave your issues at the door."

"My issues?" I spat. "You're the one who started this!"

Storm scoffed. "If you say so."

"I didn't just *say* so." I told him. "You're the spoiled brat who ruined my life!"

Storm didn't so much as wince when I said those words. He merely leaned forward, locked eyes with me and rested his elbows on his knees.

"I didn't kill your father." He growled. "I didn't and I'm sick of you acting as if I did."

I wanted to knock him out. All I could do was chew on the insides of my cheeks.

"You auditioned for a gay, romantic comedy." He pointed out. "Someone was going to be casted as your lover, a stranger."

I couldn't think of a comeback fast enough.

"But that's beside the point." Storm continued while I struggled for something scathing to say. "The rule is— Seua need a senior to take one of the lead roles. Since I'm the only one in the club with any acting experience, it only makes sense."

"What about P'Kai?"

He shifted in his seat to rest his elbows on the arms of his chair. "You'd rather kiss P'Kai? I'll be sure to let him know."

"Don't be an ass."

"What do you want me to say?" Storm demanded.

Silence.

"Were you dreaming of me?" Storm asked.

When I looked at him, he wasn't looking at me.

"What?" I asked.

"You were whispering my name." He looked up at me then. "Were you dreaming of me?"

I walked away from him to pace one way, then the next.

Yes, I was dreaming of him.

I was dreaming of things that I had no right imagining. The scary part of the whole situation was, even when I was awake, I ached for things from Storm that terrified me.

I could never admit this to him—ever. It would break my soul and betray my father.

I didn't want to answer that question. It would get me in trouble with my conscience and him. As I tried coming up with an answer, I exhaled in relief as a knock sounded at the door.

"I wanted to—" Storm frowned but he left me to check who it was and returned with Seua following him.

Clasping my palms in front of my face, I greeted him as my senior. "P."

He smiled and patted my shoulder.

"What are you doing here?" I asked him.

"I wanted to see how you were, Nong." Seua told us. "I thought you'd be in bed with your girlfriend taking care of you."

I glanced up to Storm who turned his back to walk over to the sofa. Seua followed and fell into the seat beside him.

"I feel better." I lied.

My head still felt a little weird.

"I didn't expect you to faint when I announced the roles." Seua told me. "You auditioned for Dae."

"I was just surprised, that's all." I managed.

"Surprised you got the role?" Seua asked.

"No." Storm told him. "He hates me. So, the surprise is that I'll be playing his lover."

"Um…" Seua looked from me to Storm. "So, Gift was right that you are *really* feuding."

"It's not a feud, per se." Storm explained. "I'm not the one with the issue."

"Look, I feel as if the two of you could have amazing chemistry on the screen." Seua explained. "There are moments when the characters will be angry at each other and the dislike the two of you seem to have for each other could work well with that. But if the two of you can't pretend to actually like each other, this will not work."

"What are you saying, P?" I asked.

"I'm saying, the two of you need to get it together or tell me now so I can make other plans." Seua was serious. "Keep in mind there are two love scenes. You both need to be fine with that."

"I'm fine with it." Storm shrugged.

"I can be a professional." I explained.

"It's not about being professional." Seua stressed. "Not really. The attitude the two of you have with each other is stressing me out."

I hung my head.

"This is my last film before I graduate, and I can't have it flop." Seua looked from me to Storm. "Storm, I trust you with everything. Can you do this?"

"Pretending is something I do very well, you should know this."

Seua smiled. "We're going to talk about that later. Listen, Nong, pretending shouldn't be hard. You're an actor. I want to make a film that is beautiful and believable. These two characters fall in love with each other and they're sensual with each other, kind. I need to be able to watch the two of you on that screen and believe it."

"I can do it." I pushed. "I can."

We settled into discussing some of what was to be expected over the next few weeks.

"I don't want this to be about sex." Seua explained. "It's about sensuality."

"What's the difference?" I wanted to know.

"Storm, stand." Seua said as he rose to his feet.

Without warning, he grabbed Storm by the hair and Storm slipped to his knees.

"This, is sex." Seua told him.

He then slipped to his knees in front of Storm and framed his face tenderly.

The way Storm looked at him then made me jealous. I knew it was only for show, to teach me a lesson, but Storm's bedroom eyes—I wanted them on me.

"This is sensuality." Seua added.

"Oh." I trembled.

"I want when the two of you look at each other, I want to feel it—not see it."

I blushed.

"We will have a few rehearsals where I will have small workshops to get you guys close." Seua told me. "I'm hoping that will help. Good?"

"Good." My voice cracked.

Seua nodded, patted Storm's shoulders and left us alone.

When Storm turned to look at me, I picked up my phone and exited the dorm to find a quiet place to sit so I could think.

The next meeting, I called Storm to the side and paused to gather my thoughts before meeting his eyes. "I want this to work for Seua." I admitted. "Can we call truce for now?"

"Truce?" Confusion filled Storm's eyes. "I didn't—"

"You do know what that word means, right?"

"I wasn't fighting with you, Wind." Storm told me. "I never want to fight with you. I get you don't want me around, but I graduate soon. I need all of this so I can get out of here. All I need for you to do is play along—I'll be out of your way soon enough."

That thought sent sadness through me and I wasn't sure why hearing that didn't make me happy. I rested my hand on my hips but before I could speak again, Gift interrupted, telling us the meeting was about to begin.

"You're up to it," I said in front of Gift. "We could go away together."

"Away." He blinked. "Together?"

"Yeah—maybe I could take you home." I shrugged. "This would give us some time together—to feel each other out. See if we can get along."

"How is that a good idea?" Gift stepped in. "And there are no hotels in your village."

"You can stay with me at Mae's." I didn't take my eyes off Storm.

"Your mother—" Storm rubbed the back of his neck. "I can barely deal with you and your—"

"My mother doesn't hate you." I promised. "She'll welcome you."

"You're asking me to go home with you?" Storm's voice was soft.

"Wind, P'Storm is used to luxury." Gift piped up. "What's it going to be like for him staying at your place?"

"What is your point?" I snapped.

"He won't be comfortable." Gift replied.

"Could you stay out of this, please?" I snapped at her. "I'm trying to make this work. If we can't get along, P'Seua is going to hurt and it's not fair to him."

"I'm only trying to help." She pouted.

"You're not helping." I frowned. "Back off."

"Wind," Storm said.

"I know." I sighed. "But she really isn't helping. What do you think of the idea?"

"I think it's a great idea." Storm's voice cracked. "I'd love to see where you live and meet your mother."

My cheeks flushed because he didn't look away as he said that. His voice dropped to a low, sexy drawl that made every part of me pulse.

"Think it over a little more and let me know." Storm continued. "I want you to be sure."

"Mmm."

But we didn't go in right away. Storm caught my arm as I walked by him.

"You're serious about us going away, right?"

I nodded.

He released my arm and left to enter the space in front of us.

"What was that about?" Gift asked as she wrapped her arm with mine to escort me back in the theatre space.

"Nothing." I lied, pulling my arm from her.

"You're taking him home?" Gift didn't get the idea. "You're taking him home to your mother."

"What's that supposed to mean?" I asked her.

"You only take someone home like that is if you're dating." She grunted.

"You don't know what you're talking about." I growled at her. "Stop."

Gift reached for my arm again, but I shrugged her off. She was too close, and I didn't want to be touched. Atop of everything else, I wasn't sure why she'd kept interrupting as I spoke with Storm.

I was getting a bad feeling in the pit of my stomach that I couldn't quite put my finger on.

I sat and set my bag beside me on the empty chair hoping Gift would get the idea and take the seat on the other side of my bag. Instead, she moved my bag to the far seat.

She kept resting her head on my shoulder which was becoming increasingly irritating.

Storm stared at us the entire time and suddenly, I didn't feel comfortable with Gift being this handsy with me while he watched.

Then it was his turn to speak about the music for the movie. As he spoke, my eyes drifted to his lips and my thoughts went back to seeing him wrapped in nothing but a towel. I thought about the rising need in me to reach forward and unhook the material to see what was beneath it—to see what I wanted.

I could see how sexy he was—his perfectly sculpted muscles, his abs, the tattoo of a bionic butterfly over his left pec. Other than the ink, his body was perfect, and I'd wanted to press my palms to his chest to see if he was as warm and alluring as he'd been in my dreams.

Was he hard and pulsing as he was in my dreams, and could he make me whimper the way I had in my sleep?

The lyrics of *Take My Body* filled my mind as well and I knew a cold shower would do nothing to help me.

Storm caught me staring and I was angry at myself at the way I blushed.

"What about the kiss scenes and love scenes?" One of the cast members asked.

"Wooo!" The others cheered.

Gift bounced me with her shoulders.

I wanted the floor to open up and swallow me whole.

"They aren't explicit." Seua explained. "It is a school film after-all. It will require some very fancy filming techniques to make it work, but I think we're capable."

With our meeting over, Gift and I decided to go out for dinner.

Thankfully, this time she didn't invite Storm.

I needed a moment away from him, to stop thinking about his beauty and the way I wanted him to touch me.

I needed space between his heated eyes and my body, to breathe and come back to myself.

If she'd invited him, I was pretty sure my body would implode.

As I walked by him in a conversation with his friends and brother, I caught his eyes. There was a look in them that threatened to blacken my very soul. But even then, I couldn't look away until a column blocked my eyes from his.

Seated in the front seat of Gift's car, I wondered what it all meant.

Maybe I should speak to my mother. That thought was quickly interrupted by my phone going off. When I checked, I half expected it to be a message from Storm.

Instead, my heart fell when I saw it was a text from Bank asking if I was free.

"*Sorry, heading out with a friend.*" I replied. "*Maybe this weekend?*"

Soon after, he replied. "*It's a date.*"

I blinked and shoved the phone into my pocket.

We parked at my dorms and crossed the lot and headed a long a walkway lined with flowers, over a footbridge that raised over a bicycle path.

Down the other side, the path led to a cute little noodle shop on the other side.

It sat between a coffee shop and a bakery that sold Thai and Japanese desserts.

As we ate, Gift chatted happily about the film. She had gotten the role of a grade schoolteacher who would become my character's best friend. That role I would have to do some serious pretending. A part of me was still unsure about her.

I didn't want to tell her any of my secrets. I was beginning to have a very bad feeling about her, and I wasn't entirely sure what that was.

When it came to the film, my excitement for the whole thing had dimmed the moment I realized I had to kiss someone else—then worn off completely when I was informed that the person would be Storm.

I was barely paying much attention to anything else but my dread of those kisses and going back to the dorm after dinner.

"I know the two of you don't get along." Gift was saying when I shook my head and picked up my drink. "Are you going to be able to do this?"

"Do what?" I asked.

"Two kiss scenes, a love scene—the closeness. The intimacy."

I offered a one shoulder shrug though inside my head was screaming for me to back out and join a different club. But I had promised I wouldn't let Seua down. There had to be another way of doing this film without completely losing my mind about the closeness to Storm.

"The kisses aren't real, anyway." I pointed out.

"I knew that." She huffed. "But you're going to have to put your mouth on him—do you really want to do that?"

"It doesn't matter. We kiss people all the time. Why should this be any different?"

"It *is* different." Gift stressed.

"You're supposed to be encouraging me with this!" I pointed out. "You're my friend, remember? This role is important to me—it's important to P'Seua."

"What about me?"

"What about you?" I grumbled.

"This is important to me too." Gift pointed out after a suspicious pause.

"You don't have to kiss the guy you hate, do you?"

"Why are the two of you the way you are anyway?" Gift countered.

By then I was just over the day and everyone I'd come across in it. "I don't really want to talk about it."

She seemed shocked then offended that I would refuse to explain but I was at the point where I didn't care.

Gift was a little quieter for the rest of dinner and even on the walk back to her car. I walked her to her car only because it was expected. But the moment she started the engine, I shoved my fingers into my pockets and made my way toward my dorm.

After checking the time, I realized I had at least two hours before I had to be inside.

The air had cooled down and since I wasn't a fan of the artificial air in the room, I sat on the front steps, texting back and forth with Bank who was freaking out about an essay we had to do for English.

I promised I'd have some time the next day to help him with some of it.

He promised to bring me snacks as a thank you.

I smiled and shook my head.

When I put the phone away, I lifted my eyes to the sky just as a light streaked across it.

Though I wasn't sure what it was, I tried thinking of a wish to make, just in case it was a shooting star.

I couldn't come up with anything.

Though a small voice told me I should wish for Storm to go away, the thought of waking up and not seeing Storm or have him not come back to the dorm made me sad.

Frowning, I got up and picked up my bag.

When I did enter our room, Storm was busy, his headphones on, going through the script with a red pen. I had yet to even crack the seal. I had been too terrified to see where the kisses land or the love scene was.

It wasn't as if I could avoid it.

I set my bag on the floor, pulled out my chair and turned it to face him. When he didn't look at me, I waved my hand in front of his face to get his attention. Storm removed his headphones and offered me his attention.

"Can we talk?" I asked.

"This is new." The hesitation was rich in his eyes.

At first, I thought he wouldn't want to. But after a while of what I could only describe as silent contemplation, Storm closed the script and turned to face me. "You want to talk? To me…"

I nodded.

"About what?"

"The script—most importantly, the love scene and the kisses."

"Of course." Storm's shoulders rose and fell heavily. "It's acting, Wind. I know you may think I don't know the difference between real and make-belief."

"That's not what I think at all."

Storm stopped short of rolling his eyes. "I won't do anything you won't approve of. It's over the moment Seua yells *cut*. We stop, life goes on."

"But—"

He uncurls himself from the bed and shook his head. "Don't worry. We won't be alone. And I'm very sure your girlfriend understands that this is just for a film and not real. I could try and explain it to her, if you'd like."

"My girlfriend?"

"That's why she was against you taking me home, isn't it?" Storm asked. "She's afraid we might get *too* close?"

"She's—"

My phone rang and before I could ask Storm to wait for a second while I fielded the call from my mother, he was already in the bathroom with the door closed behind him.

I sighed. "That went south—fast."

Storm

The rain started first thing in the morning and that restricted the things I had planned. I couldn't go for a run, so I went to school early and spent the hour before my first class in the music room. I set to work on the theme song for the film and had a basic outline before I had to go to class.

I couldn't focus there—instead, I scribbled away in my notebook, pretending to be taking notes while secretly recording my professor so I could listen and take notes later.

I avoided my friends for lunch but turning my phone off and napped in a corner of the library until it was time to tackle my other classes.

But I couldn't go the entire day without seeing the people in my life. I had responsibilities that extended outside of myself and classes.

I arrived at the theatre early and sat with my back against the wall with my guitar in my hands. I strum idly at the keys, not really playing a song, but loving the vibrations and the notes. I wasn't sure how long I had been sitting there before the door at the back of the room opened and someone stepped in.

Little by little more entered and I sighed and put away my guitar and stood in time for Kai and Gear yo arrive. I went to their side and immediately Gear had questions.

"I'm fine." I told him. "You know how I get when I start writing a new song. This one is kind of a big deal."

Kai groaned. "You could have answered our calls to let us know you were still breathing—is all we're saying."

I patted his back. "*P Kho tod,* Pa." I apologized as Wind entered.

Kai still smacked me on one shoulder while Gear punched the other. I groaned and while rubbing both spots, I returned my attention to Wind.

Surprisingly, he was alone, but I could tell by the look on his face, that he wasn't in a good mood, and I was over his attitude.

If he didn't want to be a part of the film, he can go and Seua would have to recast him.

But the more the acting workshop went on, the more irritable Wind became and the shorter my temper became. I lost my control over my temper when Seua became upset and stormed out.

"That's it!" I bellowed. "Everyone out!"

People scrambled and headed for the door, but I caught Wind's arm and shoved him roughly back into his seat.

"Not you." I told him angrily.

When the room was empty, I turned and leveled my stare on him. "You're now acting like an insolent child."

"What!"

"Don't speak!" I snapped. "Shut up and listen."

Wind didn't seem impressed with my outburst, but I didn't care.

"I'm going to give you twenty-four hours to decide if you want to do this." I told him in a low voice. "After that, I will deal with you accordingly. If you come back, we will expect you to work. If not, we find someone else. I will not let you ruin this for Seua."

"You can't give me that ultimatum." Wind snapped. "You're not the boss here. This isn't your film."

"You're right. But Seua means a lot to me. If you can't pretend, then you leave. Those are your choices." I leaned in, dangerously close. "Questions?"

When Wind said nothing, I picked up my guitar and stormed out of the room. Gift tried speaking with me, but I said nothing to her. Instead, I walked by her and headed for the exit with Gear running after me.

"What happened?" Gear asked.

"Nothing happened." I stopped to look at him. "I'm sick of his attitude. If he hates me, that's one thing, but I will burn his life to the ground if he messes this up for Seua."

"P, calm down." Gear told me. "No need to get Old Testament on the guy."

Grunting, I turned to leave again but Gear caught my arm.

"Come hang out with me tonight." Gear suggested. "We both know you're just going to go back to the dorm and be miserable. I won't invite the others—just you and me. We haven't had time together in a while."

I touched his cheek gently. No matter how angry I was, my brother always knew how to cheer me up.

"Is that a yes, P'Storm?" Gear asked.

"Did you drive today?" I asked.

"No."

"Let me guess—P'Kai drove you."

Gear's cheeks flushed a healthy pink and I smiled and wrapped my arm around his shoulders to lead him out the door toward my car.

We talked about my music, his photography and a slew of other things that took my mind off the anger I'd shown to Wind. I never wanted to be that dark cloud with him, but enough was enough.

I drove us to Gear's favorite restaurant.

After we ordered our meals, I tried being present but apparently, I failed. Gear smacked my arm to get my attention before setting his utensils on his plate to glare at me.

"This was a bad idea." Gear sighed. "You're obsessed with this *thing* with Wind. What is it about him that makes you so crazy?"

"I wanted something from him that I know now I'll never get." I admitted out loud to someone other than my grandfather. "I'm taking it a little hard, that's all."

"And I understand losing something precious." Gear leaned forward. "But do you think you can get it together so P'Seua and P'Kai can stop worrying about you? They don't need the added stress."

"Sir, yes sir." I offered my brother a mock salute.

He frowned.

"Stay?" I pleaded. "I promise to pay attention to my time with you."

Gear lounged backward in his chair and regarded me for a breath then nodded. "Fine."

I did the best I could, even having some worthwhile conversations with him.

In the end, Gear was happy, but I was still frazzled, trying to keep up with everything I now had on my plate.

With dinner done, I drove Gear to a nearby dessert place for a treat then dropped him at his Condo.

After pulling into the parking lot at the dorms, I pulled out my phone to check it. It had gone off twice along the drive, but I usually didn't check messages while driving.

"Paid band gig." Seua sent me and Kai. *"Think we can swing it? I kind of need the money."*

I agreed to it without much thinking. Seua knew my schedule better than I did and would plan things accordingly. Kai immediately agreed and I put the phone away, not having the heart to go inside.

Instead, I grabbed the blanket from the trunk and climbed into the back seat. Using my bag as a pillow, I got as comfortable as I could and closed my eyes.

The night around me was strangely quiet. The air was cool, and my body relax and pulsed into the leather under me.

I was just drifting off to sleep when someone knocked on the back window above my head. Irritated, I looked up to see Wind waving at me.

All I asked for was one night before I had to face him again.

One night to allow my anger to dissipate before tackling the subject of the film again.

When I didn't move to open the door, he knocked again.

Shaking my head, I reached over and unlocked the door, dropped the blanket on the seat and stepped out to face him. He eased back but looked up into my face with questioning eyes.

"You can't sleep here, P." He told me.

"What do you want, Wind?"

"You have a bed upstairs." He pointed out instead of answering my question. "Why are you sleeping here?"

"You know why."

Wind sighed, turned away but quickly faced me again. "I'm trying, P'Storm."

I didn't speak.

"Please, come back to the room."

I meant to walk away. But the softness in his voice, the hand he rested in the center of my chest blinded me to all reason I should still be angry.

Before I could stop myself, I had grabbed my things from the car, and he was holding my hand and leading me into the building.

Wind didn't release my hand until he stepped forward to call the elevator. Neither did he speak another word.

In our room, I placed my things down, set my laptop on my bed and went into the bathroom to wash up and change. When I returned, Wind handed me a bowl of noodles.

For some reason, I didn't have the heart to tell him I'd already eaten. I accepted it, wondering why he was suddenly being so nice to me.

While he ate, I kept my eyes on him. He didn't look up. Each time he slurped noodles into his mouth, it was after poking the food a few times with his chopsticks.

I finished what I was given, and he took the bowls back into the kitchen and didn't come back until he'd washed them. By then, I had school work out.

The heat of his stare burned into me and after a while, I couldn't stand it any longer.

"You're staring." I said without looking away from the math equations I'd been muddling through.

"*Kho tod, P.*"

"And why the honorifics all of a sudden?"

"Like I said. I'm trying." He answered. "I'm trying to look at you as my lover."

I swallowed.

Though I knew he meant his lover in the movie, my heart still did a little jolt as if it was trying to restart itself. Needing time to calm my breathing, I set my pencil in my textbook to keep my page, then turned to him.

"As your lover?" My voice had dropped to a lower octave. "And as your lover, do you like what you see, Wind?"

Wind hung his head. "Yes."

I choked.

To say I wasn't expecting that reply would have been an understatement.

He meant for the movie.

"Well, you don't have to worry." I told him. "I know you're not into guys."

Wind stared at me until I squirmed under his eyes and rose to leave for the bathroom.

Even then, he didn't try stopping me. By the time I returned, he was asleep.

I knew I wouldn't fall asleep if I tried. Instead, I sat in the center of my bed, finishing up my homework and messaging back and forth with Gear until he went silent.

I figured he passed out.

I went through the next day with some kind of normalcy. I even put some time in to play basketball with Kai, Seua, Gear and a few of Gear's friends.

The girls congregated as usual, and I frowned.

"They're hoping you'll take off your shirt, P." Gear bounced me with his shoulder to whisper to me.

"That's not going to happen." I told him.

He laughed out loud then waved at Kai to pass him the ball. I tried intercepting but he merely caught it, spun away from me and hit a perfect three-pointer.

The girls cheered.

Kai jumped on my back for me to carry him to the water and I swore all the girls swooned.

I knew pictures will be loaded all over their social media accounts even before we had time to drink an entire bottle of water to cool down.

Sweaty and tired, I went to Gear's place showered and took a nap.

At least, I intended on taking a short nap. But I guess my body had other plans.

When I woke, it was too late to head back to the dorms. I sent Wind a text letting him know I was with Gear, plugged my phone in and rolled over.

When I made an appearance to my brother the next morning, he was sipping coffee in the living room.

"Why didn't you wake me?" I asked him.

"When was the last time you slept?"

"I'm fine." I told him.

"You're not fine." Gear pushed. "You're usually a light sleeper. You fell asleep with the light on. I went into the room to turn it off. You didn't even twitch. Normally, I even breathe at your door and you're awake."

I chuckled. "I guess I was a little tired."

"P'Storm, you have to slow down." Gear advised. "I know you want to be everything to everyone, but could you just settle for being a musician, a student and my brother for a few days?"

I poured myself some coffee and sat across from him. "Do you know something I don't know?"

"P'Seua got *Base Note* a gig next weekend." Gear explained. "It's huge. Apparently, it will pay enough to for his entire final year."

I arched a brow. "Tell me more."

"Why don't you talk to him?"

"He's in meetings all day today with the school about the film." I replied. "Tell me."

Gear sipped from his mug then leaned in as if he was about to tell me the meaning of life. "There's this new hotel not far from here, on the beach. It's huge and luxurious. They are doing this concert series with local band for the next month to promote local talent. Rumor has it, the son of the man who owns it, goes to our school and he was the one who told his father about *Base Note.*"

"Do you know who the son is?"

Gear shook his head. "All that matters, is that you guys scored this job. And since you usually give Seua your share of the band's profits, he'll be able to go with us on our year end trip."

I smiled. "We may just be able to salvage this year."

Gear nodded. "And if you can score more time there, maybe that second album you guys have been talking about?"

"I don't know why they won't just let me pay for it."

Gear smiled. "Because they want to put something into it as well. How about you tell Seua, that you'll pay for the new album, if you get to keep your share of the royalties this time?"

I arched a brow—that was a good idea.

Gear grinned. "You like that idea. You like it a lot."

Not admitting anything out loud, I slurped some coffee into my mouth.

I skipped the Friday classes but met up with the band in the afternoon. Seua was bouncing off the walls and it looked as if he hadn't slept. He told us about the gig, handed us a list of songs he thought would be appropriate then sat down to listen to what we thought.

Kai suggested we test out *Remember Fireflies* and see what the audience thought and Seua happily agreed. Once Kai left to meet up with some other friends, I sat down alone with Seua.

I also tested him with the idea for the new album. After a few minutes of thinking about it, Seua agreed but only if we were paid for our gig at the hotel.

"When was the last time you slept?" I asked him.

"Can't sleep." He replied, shifting so he could stretch out and rest his head on my lap. "I'm so excited. If we can please this man, we can have a gig every month if we want it. There's a lot riding on this."

"For the next few minutes, just rest."

I stayed that way for a while with him, giving him a moment to breathe before diving back into work.

He drifted off into a nap and instead of only five minutes, I allowed him to remain that way for half an hour.

After we planned our next rehearsals, I headed back to the dorm.

"You're back," Wind said.

"Yes, I'll be away next weekend." I told him. "My band is playing somewhere."

"Mm." His reply was thoughtful. "Can I ask you something?"

I looked at him for a second before nodding.

"Your song *Take My Body*."

Wind didn't say anything afterward.

"*Khrap?*"

"Did you write that?" Wind asked.

"*Khrap.*" I nodded

"Experience?"

I smiled and remained quiet, forcing him to look up at me. When he did, Wind's cheeks were beautifully pink.

"Did you like the song?"

Wind dropped his eyes. He picked on the corners of his fingers.

I hunched in front of him, wanting to ask if he'd ever ask me to take his body. Then I remembered he was with Gift and I exhaled loudly.

"There's no shame in asking the right person to take your body, Wind." I told him. "There's no shame in being sexy for that person."

"Then why do I feel like I'm doing something wrong every time I get those thoughts?" Wind asked.

It was the first time he'd been like this with me—open, free.

I patted his knee. "We were taught that. It has been imprinted into our DNA that we should feel ashamed to be turned on by our special person. Hold no shame for wanting who you want. And if she's okay, be as wild as you want to be."

"P..."

"It's okay. No judgments here." I stood and put some space between him and I. "We all have our moments when we are in the mood."

He offered a small, nervous smile. "Oh—I'll be away as well. Gift and I are going to the beach."

"You and Gift. Right." I turned to pull my laptop from my bag and set it on my bed.

"I could cancel it to come to your gig." Wind told me. "I've never seen you play before."

"Listen, Gift is probably already irritated with us doing this film together." I scoff. "Plus, the idea of me going to your village with you. I don't want to get you into any more trouble with her."

"P—"

"We'll be posting the videos online." I interrupted. "Go on your date. You can see me play another time."

"You're disappointed in me."

I smiled and walked over to hunched down in front of him again. I stared up into his eyes. "I'm not disappointed in you. I'm trying to clear the air between us. That's all I need from you right now."

"I'm trying."

"I know."

But even though I knew, and even though I encouraged him, I knew what they would be doing on that trip, and it killed me. I knew he was asking me all those questions so he could be with her. It killed me advising him, but the right thing to do was what I had done.

Over the next week, each time I saw Wind at school, he was with Gift or another student they introduced as Bank. I wasn't upset at Bank's closeness to Wind—but watching the way Gift pawed all over Wind made me want to light the world on fire.

Bank and Wind seemed to be developing a friendship—a genuine closeness that obviously drove Gift crazy.

Each time Bank wrapped his arm around Wind's shoulder, Gift tried to squeeze herself between them. At one point, Wind's irritation caused him to walk around the table and sat on the only free bit of the seating.

Bank sat on his lap.

Gift stood to the side with her arms wrapped around herself.

I didn't understand her attitude—maybe it was because my brain was overly tired.

Maybe it was because I was jealous of the way Gift was with Wind that I was seeing jealousy everywhere.

I liked Bank immediately.

He seemed genuinely interested in learning new things.

Most often than not, whenever he came over, it was because he was being tutored by Wind.

When the weekend finally arrived, Wind left in the morning with Gift. I could hardly be angry since they were dating.

The plan was they were going to stop at a couple of classes first, then would leave from there and head straight to the beach.

We, on the other hand, had a few stops to make first.

Getting to the hotel wasn't hard. The hotel sent us a luxury bus to carry us as well as all our bags and equipment. I sat by myself close to the back, scribbling into my notebook, rehashing the pre-chorus of the theme song for the movie.

I was beginning to get nervous about it—filming began the next week after returning from our gig. We were about an hour into the ride when Gear moved back to sit with me.

He said nothing, only rested his head to my shoulder and went to sleep. At some point, my head was laid on his and I too drifted off to slumber.

But it wasn't to last—Gear woke me up with worry in his eyes. I looked up to see that Kai and Seua were also staring at me.

"What's wrong?" I asked, rubbing my tired eyes.

"You were having a nightmare." Gear replied. "And we're here."

Clearing my throat, I sat up in my seat and looked out. The sprawling hotel towered upward then spread outward looking like something out of Greek mythology.

Beautiful, white curtains flowed through the windows of the upper level, perfect white columns head up the structure and the glass windows and walls glittered in the sunlight.

Though I was still tired, the view did something to wake me up as I rose and followed my brother from the bus.

Outside, I lifted both hands above my head and pushed upward, stretching my back. Kai took the moment to massage my lower back, making me moan.

"We get to use the amenities here." Seua told us. "Maybe we could get massages."

"Yes, please." I moaned.

We made our way up the front steps to check in.

"You're the band!" The lady at the front desk cheered. "Hold on. I'll get someone to show you to your suite."

We offered her wai and sat in some of the beautiful chairs to wait. The man who arrived was familiar to us.

"Bank!" I greeted him.

"*Sawatdii khrap, P.*" He clasped his palms in front of his smiling face. "Welcome."

"What are you doing here?" Kai asked.

"My father owns the hotel, P." Bank replied.

We were stunned.

"Come on." Bank told us. "I'll show you to your suite then I have lunch set up for you so you can breathe before you check out the performance space."

"We have to unload the bus." Seua told him.

"Don't worry." Bank was already walking off toward a set of elevators. "It's being taken care of. And they will be careful."

I thanked him and followed until we arrived at a private area. When he used the card to open the door, I almost lost my breath. The space was beautiful. Seua seemed to be having a little problem accepting the space around us.

He still had problems with luxury as he didn't grow up with much.

I rubbed his back and Seua smiled at me and stepped further in.

We went down to a lovely lunch then off to see where we would be performing. When we entered the room, I couldn't help the shock.

"P!" Gear gasped, filming it all. "This is bigger than anywhere you've ever performed before."

"Bank, are you sure you want us?" Kai asked.

"I'm sure." Bank replied. "My dad's assistant handled getting the bands. I didn't know you were one of the ones chosen until about ten minutes before you arrived. My father realized you were students at my school."

I climbed up to the stage where our equipment was now stored. I found my guitar and sat on the edge of the stage, wondering if our music was good enough for such a stage.

"I've heard you guys perform." Bank explained. "You're all over YouTube. Don't worry. The crowd will love you. The tickets sold out within an hour of us announcing *Base Note* would be here. An hour!"

"We won't let you down." Seua promised.

"*Susu na?*" Bank beamed.

Wind

The smell of the sea air always left me calm. It cleared my mind and allowed me to think things through a lot more carefully. While Gift slept, I climbed out of the sofa, folded the sheet and changed into a pair of track pants and a graphic shirt.

After gathering a keycard, I let myself out of the bedroom. I wandered out a backdoor that led along an intricately decorated hall, down some steps and along the beach. Thankfully, I was alone. It seemed everyone else knew what vacation meant except me.

But I needed the peace and quiet.

At a particularly quiet part of the beach, I sat in the sand and stared out over the water. As I sat there, my mind wandered to my father, the happiness he always felt when on a beach, his toes under the sand and the water around his ankles.

I remembered as a child being tossed up and caught over the water. The first wave that ever hit me, happened in his arms. The safety I felt then had me laughing happily, my tiny arms tangled around his neck.

My father was my hero and now I was fantasizing about the guy who caused me not to be able to say goodbye to this hero.

My heart raced thinking about Storm.

My whole body had a beautiful reaction to his frame.

Just thinking about the tattoo on his chest, the perfection of his abs, the way his eyes raged when he looked at me in the theatre—I grew hard.

Being turned on by Storm wasn't the thing I should ever do.

But it didn't get any better. The idea he wrote *Take My Body*, made my arousal even worse.

I licked my lips, pressed my thighs together and groaned.

Sitting on the beach cleared my mind enough for me to realize that I had a thing for Storm, that I felt for him things my mother felt for my father.

I felt that blinding attraction that had me touch myself the night before in the shower, of feeling my body shudder and explode as his smile rushed through my mind.

The very thought of how good it felt as he cared for me sent my heart pulsing in a way only he could.

I tried telling myself it was only a crush—that people had them all the time.

But who was I trying to fool?

Realizing I wanted Storm in all the ways that should matter sent guilt surging through my veins like oxygen.

"Pa, what do I do?" I asked, looking up at the sky. "Tell me what to do?"

I'd wanted to talk to Gift about what I had been feeling. But she'd been acting strangely of late.

That and I still had that bad feeling in the pit of my stomach especially with what happened before we left the campus.

Storm had been by to see me before we left on the road trip to the hotel. I saw him enter the room and exited again before climbing into Gear's car and they headed off.

There was no reason for Storm to really go to the business department. He was a music student and hadn't been taking any courses at my campus.

When I asked Gift why Storm had been there, she said she hadn't seen him.

She could've been telling the truth, but something in me told me she was lying.

Curious, I sent a text to Storm.

"P, you didn't say goodbye."

It took a few minutes but eventually my phone sounded.

"*I tried. You weren't there and I didn't have time to look for you. I gave your girlfriend a note.*"

I winced.

Hearing him call Gift that bothered me. But each time I tried explaining otherwise, something always got in the way.

A note—I only thought the two of them spoke. Angry, I went back to the hotel to find Gift yelling at a hotel staff. I stepped in to find out what was happening as the poor girl bowed repeatedly while apologizing.

"That's no reason to be yelling, P." I told her.

Turning to the girl, I smiled at her. "It's fine." I promised her. "Please inform the kitchen they gave you the wrong order and bring the proper one here. Don't be flustered."

She nodded at me and scrambled from the room.

"What's the matter with you?" I demanded. "You do not speak to working people like that."

"People like that are incompetent." Gift snapped.

For some reason, she seemed to be in a horrible mood, but I didn't care. After washing my hands, I went back to pour myself some juice then turned to face her while she picked through a bowl of fruits.

"My mother is *people like that*." I reminded her.

She didn't reply but tucked a wayward strand of black hair behind her ear and went back to the fruits.

"Did you see P'Storm before we left?" I asked.

"You already asked me that." She didn't look away from her snack. "I already told you I didn't."

"You're lying."

Gift sputtered. "How dare you!"

"Did you think P'Storm wouldn't tell me?" I asked. "Storm left a note with you for me. Where is it?"

She took her fruits and tried leaving but I grabbed her arm.

Gift slapped me across the face, but I didn't release her arm. She tried tugging away—I held her tighter.

"Where is it?"

"I ripped it up!" She snapped. "He's leaving notes for you now? Why?"

"That is none of your business!" I informed her. "What did it say?"

She said nothing.

"What did it say?"

"I don't remember."

I shook her. "You're lying again!" I snapped. "What did it say!"

"You're hurting me!"

"Good!" I told her. "I'm sick of people lying to me. Tell me what it said."

"I don't remember!"

I released her and shook my head.

"You're starting a fight?" She demanded. "With me? I could kick you out of this room right now and you'd have nowhere to stay or you won't have a way of getting back to university. Think about that."

Her words stunned me into silence.

Gift folded her arms across her chest and lifted her chin. "If I were you, I'd show me some respect."

Shaking my head, I tossed what was left of my drink into her face.

She gasped. "This is Gucci!"

Instead of answering her outburst, I dropped the glass to the floor and sauntered into the bedroom to shove my things into my bag. She rushed in after me, trying to stop me from packing, while apologizing.

I didn't want to hear it. It wasn't that she threw her money in my face that made me livid.

It was the fact Storm had thought enough of me to leave me a note. He didn't have to, especially with how I'd been behaving toward him. He'd thought of me to drive to my department to see me before leaving.

It was my fault I was late. It was my fault not telling Storm where I would be that day before we were both supposed to leave the city for the weekend.

"You're really leaving?" Gift asked. "Where are you going to go?"

"That's not your concern." I told her.

"Seriously, Wind."

"Get out of my way." I walked around her.

"I shouldn't have said that!" She told me, pulling my shoes from my bag.

I pushed her away, retrieved my extra pair of shoes and put it back in my bag. Though I didn't say anything to her, Gift kept right on speaking.

Even as I headed for the door, she tried pulling me back, begging me not to go. But I opened the door, stormed out and crashed into someone heading down the hall.

"*Pom kho tod.*" I apologized while trying to pick up my bag.

The person retrieved my phone from where it had skidded and as I stood, extended it out to me.

"P'Wind!" Bank cheered.

Gift stopped speaking as she glared at Bank.

"Bank." I arched a brow. "What are you doing here?"

"I didn't tell you?" Bank asked. "My father owns the hotel. I didn't know you'd be here."

"I'm not—not anymore." I told him. "I'm trying to find a ride back to the dorms."

"Already? It's Saturday. We have a concert tonight and it's going to be amazing. Why don't you stick around?"

"I don't have anywhere to stay right now." I advised him. "I don't want to be a bother for anyone."

"Well, that's dumb." Bank wrapped an arm around my shoulder. "Of course, you have a place to stay. And if at the end of the weekend you still need a ride, I have a car."

"Bank."

"Don't even worry about it." Bank grinned at me.

"Are you like the best friend in the world?"

He laughed. "I'm earning that title with you—I'm determined."

I bounced him with my shoulder.

"Now." Bank leaned close to me. "I have an entire two-bedroom suite to myself. And you're not a bother. Say yes."

I glanced over at Gift and knew if she was a cartoon character, she'd be smoking out the ears. With her arms folded across her chest, her eyes held a rage I couldn't understand.

"Say yes." Bank pushed. "I could get you backstage to meet some of the bands."

I nodded. "*Okay, khrap.*"

Bank took my bag, greeted Gift as if she was an afterthought then led me to his room to dump my things before inviting me to have breakfast with him.

Even as I ate, I was still wondering what was in the note. Tempted to ask Storm, I cleared my throat and refocused on Bank. He introduced me to his father who arrived to eat with us.

I could believe they were related. They had the same dark, mischievous eyes, the same nose that shaped down the center of their faces and formed into a perfect tip at the end.

They laughed the same and their smirked tugged at the corners of their lips but came to life in their eyes.

"You've never brought a boyfriend home before." His father told Bank.

"Pa!" Bank blushed. "P'Wind is not my boyfriend. He's a good friend."

His father arched a brow. "No? This is Wind, correct?"

We both nodded.

"The same Wind you said was kind to you." His father asked. "Who helped you with passing your last English test, the one you said was very smart and handsome?"

"Pa!" Bank buried his face in his hands.

I laughed and patted his shoulder. "It's okay."

"And supportive." The older man added. "How could he not be your lover?"

"Because he doesn't like guys." Bank's face was so red, it began radiating to his ears. "I asked you not to embarrass me, Pa."

"*P, Kho tod.*" His father smirked.

He wasn't sorry at all.

I could see he was trying to set his son up.

I laughed softly while sipping from my drink.

It was hard not to like Bank's father immediately, or his sister who sauntered into the private dining room, flopped at the table with a pout to ask Bank how it was that all his friends looked like models.

She introduced herself as P'Pretty and that she was Bank's older sister.

"The gorgeous one." Pretty was sure to inform me.

I offered her wai.

"And I'm the smart one." Bank stuck his tongue out at her. "Beauty fades."

"Pa!" Pretty pouted.

"Children, behave." Their father picked up a piece of fish and set it into a bowl for Pretty to eat. "Or you're both out of the will."

Bank and Pretty looked at each other, then proceeded to plead with their father who then laughed until he snorted.

I spent the day in Bank's room afterward working on the script, trying to learn my lines.

I fought hard not to focus on the kisses and the love scene. It was terrifying since I had yet to share my first kiss with anyone.

At first, I was saving it for someone special, but as I grew older, who was I really fooling?

I hadn't been kissed yet because I was terrifed of the intimacy required. My first kiss couldn't be with Storm—he'd be sure to tease me about it until I died.

Eventually, Bank returned to the room.

His father dismissed him to relax and stopped hovering. Bank fell into line helping me memorize my lines.

"You get to kiss P'Storm?" Bank's eyes widened. "I supposed it could be worse—P?"

"Hmm?"

"You aren't against—well, I know you heard what my father said." Bank explained. "I know you said nothing while with my father, but if you wanted to talk about it."

"It's no trouble." I walked over to the set up to pour myself some water. "I like guys too."

"You do, P?" Bank asked, rushing over so I had to look at him. "You aren't just saying that?"

"I'm not just saying that." I assured him.

"Don't worry—all I need from you is a friendship," he said. "My father is trying to find me someone. I understand what he's trying to do, but I don't feel that way about you. I'm sorry."

I laughed. "I don't feel that way about you either—can I ask you a question?"

"Sure, P."

"Have you ever kissed a guy?"

Bank nodded.

We went to sit on the balcony, to enjoy the natural breeze.

"I started dating someone when I was sixteen." Bank confessed. "Pa didn't like him and at first, I thought it was because I was gay. Then I thought it was because he was my father and didn't think anyone would be good enough for me. When I finally got the courage to talk to Pa about it, I realized it was because my father suspected that this guy was after me for my money."

"Please tell me your father was wrong."

"He wasn't." Bank rubbed his eyes then looked at me. "We broke up—it didn't end well. I found out the same night I—"

"Slept with him."

Bank nodded. "He was my first and for a long while I hated giving myself to someone who didn't even care about me."

I rubbed his back.

"Why do you ask?"

"I haven't kissed anyone before." I admitted. "And I will have to kiss P'Storm for this film."

Bank nodded, stroking his chin in that thoughtful way men usually did. "It doesn't have to be all bad."

"How can this be good?" I pleaded.

"Well—um—P'Storm looks like he knows how to kiss." Bank's cheeks flushed.

So did mine.

"It could be a great first kiss." Bank continued. "Mine was sloppy and awkward. I wish I'd saved it for someone who truly cared for me."

"P'Storm doesn't care for me."

"Are you sure?" Bank asked. "I mean, the first time I met him, I'm pretty sure he thought you and I were dating, and he was jealous."

I scoffed. "You're seeing things. Let's get ready for the concert."

"I'm serious." Bank caught my arm. "I had my arm around your shoulder, remember? Then he looked at me and I lowered it."

I didn't believe that. Storm had never showed any carnal interest in me. The whole time he was there, with me, taking care of me, it was because he was trying to make amends.

Somehow, I managed to change the subject.

As night fell, Bank allowed me to borrow one of his shirts to go with a black pair of pants. When I ducked into the bathroom to him fixing his hair, he stopped me, turned me to face the mirror and did my hair as well.

I stared at myself in the mirror.

I liked the way I looked, my hair slicked back, and the top two buttons of my shirt undone was a kind of sex appeal I never knew I had.

"I didn't know I was capable of looking like this." I managed. "I've never had a reason to really dress up."

"Told you the girls in that Facebook group was right."

I groaned.

"Are you ready?" Bank stood behind me.

I nodded, meeting his eyes in the mirror. "Ready.

Partying with the rich and famous was very different. I was used to small village gathering where we had to play our own music if the satellite gave out.

Gatherings where everyone I the village brought a meal and we sat around talking.

This was on a whole other level.

Everything was a lot more decadent and louder, which I realized, wasn't really my thing.

Bank introduced me to other young people my age— the son of an actor here, the daughter of a popular engineer there, the step-son of a Korean pop-icon there.

I was respectful, but the wallet size of the people around me threatened to bury me.

One band performed.

I barely paid any attention.

Eventually, Bank led me through the crowd to the front row and we flopped down in chairs beside Pretty, whose boyfriend was there, arm wrapped around her shoulder as she snuggled into his side.

"Please welcome—" The announcer was saying after I offered them wai and turned to look at the stage. "*Base Note!*"

I blinked and looked over at Bank.

He nodded. "You didn't know they were here?"

"No." I shook my head and leaned in to speak in Bank's ear as the crowd around us erupted in cheers.

I knew he had a gig somewhere, but I hadn't been interested enough to ask where.

One by one, the bandmembers made their way onto the stage.

Kai.

Seua.

Storm.

I saw Gear worming his way toward the front to snap pictures as the members got ready.

Seua went behind the drums while Kai and Storm strung their guitars over their heads and plucked a few random strings.

Storm stood at the microphone for the lead singer, and I held my breath.

"One!" Seua lifted his drumsticks above his head and banged them together. "One! Two! Three!"

I'd never heard Storm sang live before. There was no way the richness I'd heard through those headphones was the same in person.

But I was wrong.

It was even better.

The richness of his voice, the way his body moved behind the guitar, the way he interacted with the audience.

He was sexy—genuinely sexy and every part of my body was there for it.

Take My Body live was better than any aphrodisiac.

It was about making love to a lover—a lover who wanted it, who yearned for it, who couldn't get enough of it.

I bit into my bottom lip and held my breath. During Kai's guitar solo, Storm did a little dance—I didn't think a man's body could move like that. He was fluid like water and every sway of his hips made me moan.

Thankfully, the cheering fans drowned out my carnal sighs.

By the end of that song, the audience was going absolutely out of their minds.

The next song was one to dance to—one I wished I was dancing with Storm to.

Suddenly, not being in his arms angered me.

As I pressed my thighs together, it was then that our eyes met and for a second, I could have sworn he would have stopped the show in the middle of everything.

Instead, he kept my eye contact until it was time for his guitar solo. He walked away from his microphone to kneel in front of me, did his solo then stood and walked backwards to his microphone.

"I'm going to guess P'Storm did not know you were here." Bank asked close to my ear.

"He does now." I gasped.

Every part of me was aroused and I crossed my legs to hide the tent that was slowly forming in the front of my pants.

"If the two of you are going to battle," Bank said. "We have a Muay Thai gym in the south end. That should minimize the damage."

"We're not going to battle. We're not dating. I can go wherever I want."

"Did you tell P'Storm that?"

I grunted. "Can you get me backstage?"

"What kind of question is that?" Bank asked. "Are you going to fight or make love?"

"Is there a difference?"

"I see you like it rough." Bank chortled.

"Bank!"

He laughed. "Come on."

I followed him along the aisle back to the front, across the lobby then in through a side door. A guard was there but didn't try stopping us. When we dipped into the dimly lit area backstage, I tripped over myself a couple of times but caught myself against Bank.

"Be careful, P." Bank whispered.

By the time *Base Note* exited the stage, Bank and I were seated in their dressing room. Bank sat back, arms stretched along the back of the sofa and legs crossed while I paced. The band entered the room, the excitement palpable.

All of them, except Storm, greeted Bank and I with happy cheers as Gear snapped a few pictures. Storm on the other hand set his guitar across his dress table and fell into one of the other sofas while reaching for a bottle of water.

"This was where you were coming with Gift?" He finally asked.

"Mmm." I answered. "I didn't know this was where your gig would be."

"I left you a note." Storm replied. "I told you where I would be."

"I'm sorry, P." I exhaled. "I didn't get that note. I don't know what it said."

"I see." Storm lifted the water to his lips. "I take it you're staying in the same room as she is."

"Don't have a choice." I began.

"He's staying with me." Bank spoke up.

I wanted the floor to open up and swallow me whole.

Storm's fiery eyes shifted from Bank to me, then back to Bank.

"Before you blow up this hotel." Gear spoke. "Can I get a picture with the entire band?"

Storm looked over at his brother and agreed. I stepped out of the way for the band members to set up for Gear to fire off a few shots. He then had me take a picture so that he could be in it. Once they were finished, Kai, Seua and Gear left to give us some privacy.

Bank wanted to leave as well but Storm shook his head.

"There's no need. I'll leave." Storm told us.

"P'Storm." I sighed. "I didn't have a choice. Gift and I got into a fight over your note. She all but told me to find another room and a way home."

"It doesn't matter—you're staying in my room now." Storm told us, glaring at Bank. "Please have his things moved."

Bank nodded.

"Wait a minute!" I protested. "I can't just sleep with you."

"Very good choice of words, N'Wind." Storm stepped in close. "But I guarantee this—you can."

I caught my breath and tried putting some distance between us. But there was a wall behind me.

"Want to rethink that?" Storm asked.

"You know what I mean."

"Do I?" Storm smirked and stepped even closer as his hot breath bathed my face.

His eyes dipped down to my lips, and I tried putting more space between him and myself—forgetting the wall.

But he didn't let up.

He didn't seem to care Bank was still in the room.

I moved backward until my back crashed into a wall again and I gasped. "P."

"You're staying with me." Storm's voice was hard. "Questions?"

Trembling, I shook my head.

"Good." Storm stepped back to drink an entire bottle of water.

Storm

I was creating the final notes for the movie's theme song when Wind walked out of the bathroom. He had a towel around his neck and his hair was still wet.

Setting my guitar aside, I extended a hand to him. To my surprise, he accepted, and I pulled him to sit on the floor between my legs.

I then hurried into the bathroom for the hair dryer, reclaimed my position and began drying his hair. Neither of us said anything to each other and my heart raced in a nervous way I was beginning to understand. No one else made me feel that slight flip each time I thought of him.

But the hair drying process took less time than I thought and all I could do was turn off the dryer and brought it back to where I'd found it.

"P?"

"Mm."

"The note you left with Gift." Wind began. "Why didn't you just send me a text?"

"My phone was dying." I replied. "It I didn't get around to putting on the car charger yet."

"Oh." Wind answered. "What did it say?"

"You really didn't get it?"

I shook my head.

"Then it wasn't important." I told him.

"It is." Wind caught my shoulder. "Trust me when I say, it was important."

I looked at him over a shoulder. "I wanted to let you know I'd be at this hotel. To tell you it was work—I didn't want you to worry."

"You were concerned for me?"

It was hard admitting that.

"It's okay." Wind told me. "I have the answer. Can we talk?"

I nodded again.

We changed clothes and wandered from the room.

The others hadn't returned to the suite yet, so I sent Gear a message to let him know I was wandering away from the hotel with Wind.

Gear merely sent me a winking emoji and I walked beside Wind from the hotel and along the beach, enjoying the cool air.

"I think the first thing I need to tell you is that I haven't yet had my first kiss." I admitted.

"Why are you telling me this?"

"Because I think you need to know why I'm so reluctant and nervous." Wind explained. "It's silly and you're going to laugh but I have to say it. It wasn't like I've had many chances of being with someone. But I wanted to share my first kiss with someone who cared for me. Is that too much to ask."

"No."

"And you're laughing at me."

"I'm not laughing." I assured him. "Well, that shouldn't be a problem. You have a lover. She can help you with that, so you don't have to give your first kiss to me."

"It's not that simple."

"How about this?" I asked. "The kisses you share with me on set doesn't count. They are for a pretend, nothing to do with love or the need to be kissed."

"It doesn't work like that." Wind chuckled softly. "I know what you're trying to do."

"Take it from me. A kiss without feelings means nothing."

Wind sighed.

Without thinking, I curled my fingers against the back of his neck and pulled him into my chest.

Wind stiffened against me, but the moment I pressed my lips to his ear, he gripped my hips and melted into my chest.

With my free hand at my side, I dropped my lips to his shoulder. "Breathe, Wind. I'm not as scary as you think I am. I promise."

Wind sighed.

"Do you want to go back to Bank's room?"

"No." He told me, pressing his forehead to my chest. "I feel safe with you."

"Safe? In my room or in my arms like you are right now."

"Both."

I moaned, wanting to lift my head so I could kiss him. But I let him go. I didn't want to be the other man, the man who broke up what he had with Gift.

Wind looked up at me with the kind of stare that threatened to take away what was left of my fragile control.

He framed my cheeks with his palms and lifted his mouth toward mine, but I stopped him.

Pushing him away was the mantra that played in the back of my head. With each inch he drifted closer, the voice became softer and softer.

Just as our lips were about to meet, one of our phones began ringing.

For a moment, we froze like that.

It rang louder and we jerked apart.

It was Gift calling Wind.

He ignored it and walked off toward the water.

I didn't follow him.

Instead, I remained there, watching over him, giving him time with his thoughts. I knew what would happen next. Wind would feel guilt for what almost happened. I didn't want to see that, but I remained there like some dark guardian angel, wanting to make sure he was okay.

Wind's phone rang again, and Wind hung his head.

"Do you want me to answer it?"

Wind shook his head and reached for the phone. "Yes?" He answered the phone on speaker.

"Have you forgiven me?"

"No." Wind replied stoically. "You have some nerve."

"Where are you?" She asked. "Bank said you were no longer staying with him. He wouldn't tell me where you're staying. You don't have anywhere else."

"I don't think you need to worry about that, P." Wind's sounded tired. "I'm going to hang up."

"Are you with *him*?" Gift demanded in a stiff voice. "Is that why you won't come back? He doesn't care about you! You are angry at him for a reason! Why would you run back to him?"

Wind hung up and was about to whip the phone into the ocean, but I rushed forward and stopped him.

He turned and pressed his face into my neck.

"Wind?"

"I know you don't want this." Wind managed, his hot breath tickling my skin. "P, let me stay like this for a little. Please, just hold me?"

Reluctantly, I wrapped my arms around him and rubbed Wind's back until he fisted my shirt. I lifted one hand to gently rest to the back of his head, wanting to keep him close.

We remained that way until he released my shirt and looked up at me. I thought he was ready to go in, but instead, he hugged me again, pulling in closer.

I said nothing.

When he released me again, it was to offer me a small smile and to tell me he was ready to head back. We walked back to the hotel to find Gift standing outside my door. I saw the moment Wind's peace was stolen and I drew closer to his side.

She rushed over to take his hand and Wind yanked his hand away from her.

"You need to leave." I told her.

"I'm here to see Wind, not you." She intoned.

"I know some people can't read body language." I told her. "Does it look like he wants to see you?"

Gift gasped.

I didn't care.

"P'Storm?" Wind called out to me.

"Hmm?" I looked down into his eyes.

"Can we go in?"

I took his hand while using my free one to fish my key card from my pocket. When I pressed it to the monitor, I allowed Wind to walk by me into the room.

Gift turned to follow. I stepped in and closed the door in her face.

She banged on it, catching my brother and friends' attention.

"What's going on?" Kai asked.

"I thought she was my friend." Wind muttered. "Why is she acting like this?"

"So, we don't want her here, is what you're saying." Kai wanted to know.

When Wind nodded, Kai sighed and left the suite.

I knew what he was going to do, but I didn't say anything to Wind. He was already a little frazzled and I didn't want to add to his worries.

The banging stopped.

A few minutes later, Kai returned and went back to the movie he'd been watching with the others. I walked Wind into my bedroom and tucked him into my bed after getting one of the pillows and the blanket from the living room area.

"What are you doing?" Wind asked.

"I'm going to sleep here."

"Um…there's room on the bed."

"Wind…"

"It's fine." Wind's voice cracked. "Please."

My body wanted to. My mind screamed that I shouldn't, but I did it anyway.

I climbed into the bed and stretched out on my back.

Wind rolled over on his side to face me and closed his eyes.

The time ticked by as I looked down to where my hand was next to his. I wondered what Wind would do if I reached over and lace my fingers with his.

When his nightmares began, I took his hand. I squeezed it and Wind calmed down after shuffling over to rest his forehead on my shoulder.

I pressed a kiss to his forehead, allowing the warmth of it to imprint on my lips.

"I won't leave you, Wind." I assured him.

Weak, I remained in that position, holding his hand with his head on my shoulder.

If this was all I could get from Wind, I would take it.

I would take this little thing and be satisfied.

We left Wind asleep the next day to speak with Bank and his father. I was up before Wind and ordered room service. While the others ate, I shared out some food for him. Back in my room, I stared down into his handsome face for a while, then set the tray on the the bedside table.

While I waited for my friends and brother to shower, eat and dress, I stretched out beside Wind, watching his face.

He seemed rested, calmer—but then again, he was sleeping. I caressed his cheek until Wind opened his beautiful eyes and smiled at me.

My heart skipped a beat before reality kicked in by Seua walking in to tell me it was time to go.

"I have a meeting." I told him. "Here's food—I'll be back as soon as I can."

Wind nodded.

"You going to be okay?" I asked.

"Mmm."

Though I was tempted to kiss his forehead, I left the room with Seua and we headed to our meeting about the future of *Base Note* at the fancy location.

In the end, we walked away with a contract that saw us playing at the hotel once a month as well as on on Bank's and Pretty's birthday.

The father secretly thought Pretty's boyfriend would propose soon. If that happened, the music slot would be ours.

I was giddy at this good fortune—not because I needed the money, but because this could help Seua out plus *Base Note* would get some publicity from being the hotel's house band.

He gave us control over the kind of music we played but insisted that we always played *Remember Fireflies* and on Bank's birthday we play at least four of his favorite tunes.

I was pretty sure we'd just get a list of songs from Bank and play as many of them as possible.

Myself, Kai and Seua looked at each other and immediately agreed.

"I understand N'Wind is staying with you, Storm." The man told me.

I nodded.

"I would like to speak with him."

My back immediately went up.

Gear reached under the table and took my hand. Agreeing, I sent Wind a text and we took a break from the table to wait for him to arrive.

When he did, I went over to greet him, then called everyone back to the table.

"I wanted to speak with you about my son." The older man began.

"Is he okay?" Wind looked around. "Where is he?"

"He's out with his sister right now." The man smiled.

"Oh." Wind's shoulders fell as he exhaled heavily.

"Since Bank met you, he's talked of no one else. That's why I thought the two of you were seeing each other. *P kho tod.* I do want to acknowledge your friendship with him. Thank you for taking care of him. His marks in English and Literature were—dismal to say the least."

"Bank reads the books." Wind explained. "He just needed a little extra help with his tense and the like. It wasn't that big of a deal."

"Maybe not to you." He replied. "But my son is grateful. He's happier than he's been and as a father—if you need anything…"

"P. I didn't do it for something in return." Wind shook his head. "Bank's been nice. I don't get that a lot."

"I know." He smiled. "I'm just putting it out there. If there is anything you need, all you have to do is let me know."

"Thank you, P." Wind offered wai.

"Good. Now, you all can enjoy the amenities the hotel has to offer until you must leave to go back to school." The man smiled brightly. "This weekend has been a great success."

That excited us and after we packed all our things, we wandered the beautiful grounds.

Gear was in awe, taking pictures of everything.

Kai found a dessert pop-up cart and got all his favorite sweets.

Seua took a quiet moment to stare out at the water while Wind played in the water.

"I've been wondering what the deal was with the two of you." Seua spoke.

Pretty splashed Wind who squealed while trying to dodge the droplets.

Their laughter rippled back to us, warming my soul.

"I was the reason he couldn't say goodbye to his father." I admitted out loud to someone other than my grandfather.

"How so?"

"It was my birthday." I cleared my throat as my voice hitched. "The trucks carrying equipment for it was blocking a shortcut to his home. He had to take the long way—by the time he got there, his father was gone."

"And he blames you," Seua said.

I nodded. "He isn't wrong. After a few days I realized what had happened and I set out to make things right anyway I could. In the process, I fell for him. The thing is, I've had to give up on that—he's with Gift."

"I would think after what has happened those two aren't together anymore."

"Like I said."

Wind called out to me. I smiled and waved.

"I'm not the one to make Wind happy." I continued. "I'll only remind him about his father, and it will always make him sad or worse—break his heart."

"I'm sorry."

I exhaled loudly, patted his shoulder, and rose to join the others in the water. I caught Wind around the waist, and it did my heart well hearing Wind's laughter before Bank splashed me.

The battle began.

At one point, I looked up toward the hotel to see Gift watching us. While I should have been worried, I couldn't get myself to care.

Bank picked me up and tossed me into a wave.

When I surfaced again it was to find all three of them laughing.

They ran when I reached for them and I caught Wind in my arms, picked him up and twirled him into the wave.

By the time we made it back to the hotel, we had an hour to change, gather the rest of our things, say goodbye to Bank and Pretty and ensured we had everything. Bank walked us out to the bus, his arm around Wind's hip.

"Jealous?" Gear asked close to my ear.

I squinted at him which only made him laugh.

"Everyone, stand against the bus!" Gear called. "I want a picture of all of us!"

We scrambled to do what he said while he set up the camera on a tripod. He then ran toward us, tripped over himself and landed in Kai's arms.

The camera flashed then, and we all groaned. Gear went back to rest it and this time, managed to get to Kai's side before it flashed.

The drive back to school landed us back late. We were dropped off one by one and by the time Wind and I dragged ourselves back to our dorm, all I wanted to do was crawl into bed.

I knew morning would be there too soon.

Wind showered first and when I was finished and walked out with a towel around my shoulders, he was asleep. I pulled his sheets up to his shoulders, plugged in his cell to charge then went back to do the same to mine.

I was awoken in the middle of the night by an ass in my groin, a back flush against my chest, a head on my arm with hair tickling my nose. I didn't have to open my eyes to know who it was. I remembered Wind's smell and had to lean my hips away so he wouldn't know just how deeply he affected me.

"Wind?" I groaned. "Why are you in my bed?"

"I couldn't sleep." He rolled over and snuggled closer. "When I slept with you at the hotel, I didn't have nightmares all night."

I pulled him into me and wrapped my arm around him. "Okay."

"I'm nervous about filming tomorrow."

I kissed his head. "Don't be. I'll take care of you."

But while Wind was able to go back to sleep, I wanted to remember what holding him felt like. I kept falling in and out of sleep.

By the time morning came, I was surprisingly rested and ready to face my day.

Leaving Wind for the day was a little strange.

I didn't want to.

I wanted to kiss his forehead, to hold his hand and feel him squeeze mine.

Instead, I smiled at him and backed out the door, my backpack and guitar over my shoulder. Wind blushed at me just before the door closed and I couldn't remember a time my heartbeat that fast.

The day was good—I spent my break playing basketball with my brother and friends. I stole moments to finish up the theme song then sent it over to Seua and let me know if he needed any changes.

On my second break, I stole away to the Business department and wandered around until I found Wind. The students around me, mostly the females, were whispering and pointing.

It was obvious I hadn't thought this one through. They knew my face as the lead singer from *Base Note*.

A few of them tried giving me gifts, professing their love, but I politely decline. When I met with Wind, the gasp was palpable, but I didn't care.

I walked out of the building with Bank and Wind to find a place to sit in the courtyard.

"I'm sorry." I told Wind. "I didn't think of what my coming here would do to you. I keep thinking of myself as just Storm, but as you can see…"

We looked around and people were filming us and taking pictures.

"Let's go somewhere else." Wind suggested and we gathered our things to leave.

We climbed into my car and left the campus to a remote little diner on the outskirts of town.

"I'm going to give you guys some privacy." Bank told us with a wink. "I have a friend who lives close to here."

Wind agreed before I could and once we were alone, Wind turned to face me.

"I've been meaning to talk to you about something."

"Okay?"

"I was—" Wind paused to look around before leaning forward. "Could you kiss me?"

I blinked.

"I don't want my first kiss to be something that's filmed." Wind admitted.

"I thought you didn't want your first kiss to be mine."

Wind blinked as his cheeks flushed. He looked away. "Don't make me say it."

I smiled and leaned back in my chair but was interrupted for our waitress wanting to take our orders. Once we were alone again, we returned to the conversation.

"You want me to kiss you." I cleared my throat. "Is that because you want me to, or you want to get rid of this thing you think is holding you back from the scene?"

"Does it matter?"

"Of course."

Wind rubbed his forehead then pressed his lips into a thin line before speaking. "I've been thinking about it—a lot. In fact, it's the only think I've been thinking about for days now. If you don't want to, I understand."

"Here?"

Wind blushed again. "No. I just wanted to ask since I'd gathered up enough courage to ask."

"What about your dad?"

Wind bowed his head.

"Listen, if you want me to kiss you for real, I'll kiss you." I told him truthfully. "For real. But it's going to hurt you later, where you feel guilty for doing it and it'll kill me. Do you understand?"

"I understand."

"So, take the rest of today, and think about it. And then tomorrow morning, you can tell me what your decision is."

"I won't change my mind."

"Let's eat then call Bank so we can head back." I told him.

Wind

I tossed and turned all night. But the next morning, I was up ahead of my alarm and turned it off before it sounded. Excitedly, I climbed out of bed, almost falling when my feet tangled with the sheets. I managed to catch myself by gripping onto the side table.

Pushing a big gust of breath out my mouth, I looked over at Storm's sleeping form, then grabbed my phone and hurried out into the seated area at the end of the hall to make a phone call to my mother. It was the only way I seemed to be able to get a hold of her.

When I waited until a regular time of the morning, she'd be on the road, heading to work. I hated that she had to drive back and forth, but our village didn't really have all that many jobs for her to take care of herself.

Her voice was tired and that further worried me.

"Mae, you're tired." I told her.

"I'm fine, Nong." She replied as always. "Don't worry about me. Focus on school and making friends."

"Would you consider moving away from the village if it involves a better job?" I asked.

"Of course." She replied. "The drive back and forth is very hard on me. And I don't know how much longer the jeep will hold out."

I nodded wanting to cry but managed to take a few deep breaths. "I'll see what I can find."

Mae smiled and air kissed at me.

"I'm free next weekend. I want to visit you."

"Really?" She cheered up immediately. "I'd like that. I miss you."

"I miss you too, Mae."

I went on to confide in her that Storm was my roommate. I wasn't entirely sure why I saw the need to hide that from her. When she gasped, I knew now she had something else to worry about.

"Are you going to be okay with him as your roommate?" She asked. "I know you have this dislike for him ever since your father passed."

"That's the thing that I wanted to talk to you about, Mae."

"Okay."

"He's changed." I explained. "He's been trying to be nice to me ever since I got here and all I was to him was mean. But then I realized, I wasn't mean to him because of Pa. I was because I kind of like him and I feel guilty for it."

"Sweetie, tell me why."

"Because I should hate him." I hung my head. "I should want him to hurt as much as I hurt when Pa died. But instead, I feel safe when he's around. I want to smile and be held by him."

"Have you already been *held* by him?"

"Mae!" I gasped, looking around.

"I was in love once." She giggled. "Your father was my one true love. Listen, my love, if your heart is telling you to do something, do it."

"But Pa. It was his fault I didn't get to say goodbye."

"Is that why you're angry at him?"

I said nothing.

"My love, your father died about two minutes after you hung up the phone that day." Mae explained. "That's why he called you. He didn't feel strong enough to last until you got home again. Please tell me you haven't carried this hate all this time."

"But…"

"No buts." Mae's voice cracked. "Your father tried. He wanted to see you one last time, to hold you. But while his heart was willing, his body was weak."

Tears rolled down my cheeks as I hung my head.

"There is no reason to feel guilty for liking this boy." Mae pushed. "And if you're going to have him—um—*hold* you, make sure you're ready for that."

Though I was blushing, I finished the talk with my mother and sat there in the silence of the hall, fighting the pain that now pulsed through my heart. I'd spent the last two years hating Storm and what he stood for. I'd spent that time carrying that burden, that shame.

He'd tried being nothing but good to me—tried to right a wrong I'd placed on his shoulders.

Suddenly, I couldn't breathe.

"Wind?"

My name sounded distorted. I could barely catch my breath, but I looked up through a wall of tears trying to see who was calling me.

"Are you okay?" The alien voice asked.

Somehow, I managed to nod as I began floating.

When I blinked, I was in our room, lying on his bed, with a cold towel wiping down my face.

"I didn't faint." I told him proudly.

"I know." He replied. "But it'll make you feel better."

The towel moved down to my neck—one side, then the next, before it moved under my shirt.

I caught his arm and looked up to see he was fully dressed.

Taking the rag from his hand, I placed it on the bedside table then sat up, all the while staring into his eyes as I eased closer.

His warm breath floated over my face, my lips and down my chin causing me to shiver. My eyes dropped to his lips as if having a mind of their own, and he licked his lips.

"What's your answer, Wind?" Storm's voice cracked.

"Why don't you kiss me and find out?"

Storm framed one side of my neck.

He stared into my eyes as if searching for hesitation. Even as he eased his head closer, the mere inches it took for our lips to meet, he searched my eyes.

When his lips were finally on mine, I closed my eyes and held my breath.

I wasn't sure what I was supposed to be doing. I'd seen plenty of kisses in movies, but this was different.

This was my kiss—my first kiss.

The tip of his tongue tickled my lips apart and when I did open my mouth a little, he pushed his tongue in to touch mine.

A shock of electricity surged down my spine and every part of my body came to life then.

Storm was tender, licking and sucking parts of my mouth I wasn't sure he should be—but all of it felt good. I wanted him to do it again and again.

Before I knew what was happening, I was responding to him. Though I didn't know what to do with what he'd done, my body knew. It responded to Storm's kiss making him moan before leaning back to smile at me.

"What do you think?" His voice wavered.

All I managed was a soft moan before wrapping my arms around his neck and pulling Storm back against me. I lifted my mouth to him again and Storm kissed me again.

My toes curled until I took my mouth away and dropped my forehead to his shoulder, shyness pulsing through me.

"Did I pass?" Storm wanted to know.

I giggled. "You passed."

Storm kissed the side of my head and stood. "I hate to kiss and run, but now I'm late for class."

"Oh, I'm sorry."

"Don't be." Storm smiled. "It was worth it. I'll see you later for filming?"

I nodded.

"Have a good day today."

I wasn't sure how he expected me to have a good day when all I'd be thinking about was the way he kissed me. Still, I grinned up at him and nodded—determined to do was he wished.

I watched him until he was in the galley kitchen, then listened for the door to close.

I then smiled, pulled his sheets over my head, and flopped around on his bed, happiness radiating through me like fireworks in a night sky.

To avoid being late for class myself, I hopped off his bed, made it then turned my attention to my own. I showered, dressed, grabbed an apple from the fridge then rushed off to my first class—English.

I was almost late but managed to rush through the door ahead of the professor and fell into my seat beside Bank.

"That was close." Bank leaned over to whisper.

"I have a good reason." I grinned.

Bank smiled but stared at me with suspicion.

As the class went by, we carefully passed a notebook with notes back and forth to each other.

Bank could barely contain his excitement for me.

Apparently, he'd suspected I liked Storm all along. He wasn't at all surprised that Storm knew how to kiss.

"He looks like the type." Bank wrote.

I grinned.

The end of class couldn't come fast enough, and we remained behind to speak to each other in private.

"My first kiss was nothing like that." Bank admitted. "It was sloppy, and I felt nothing."

"I'm sorry."

Bank smiled. "It's okay. I'm happy your first kiss was good. It made you feel good."

I nodded.

"Have you seen the pictures Gear posted?" Bank asked.

"Not yet."

Bank leant over to show me his screen.

They were beautiful—I focused on the two Gear had secretly taken of me while Strom was kneeling in front of me, playing his guitar.

There was no secret I was hypnotized by him. I seemed to have eyes for no one else.

"I love that one too." Bank told me. "It's one of my favorites of the two of you. The way he looks at you. It's getting hard not to be jealous of you."

I smiled. "I didn't even realize I was looking at him like that. Or that he was looking at me like that."

"Not surprised." Bank laughed.

"People in the comment section likes it too from the looks of it."

"So, you're ready for shooting this evening?" Bank asked as we left the classroom.

"Yeah." I replied. "The only thing I was worried about was the kiss."

"Now you have no worries."

"I wouldn't say I have *no* worries." I told him. "Pretending to make love to someone in front of people is still a concern. But I do feel like I'm protected when I'm in Storm's arms."

"I want that one day."

I scoffed. "You're a good-looking guy."

He flipped his hair off his forehead dramatically. "You think so?"

We burst into laughter.

"Wind?"

Good feeling gone.

"Can we talk?" Gift asked.

"Do you want me to stay?" Bank asked.

I shook my head. "No. This won't take long."

"I'm not going far." Bank eyed her.

True to form, he walked across the path to sit at a picnic table and pulled out his phone. When I turned to Gift, she sat on the wall seat behind us, and I took a spot beside her but not too close.

"What do you want?" I asked.

"I made one mistake." Gift told me. "I didn't mean to keep the note from you."

"Yes, you did." I told her. "It wasn't like you put it down and forgot it was there. You ripped it up, P."

"Can we just get past this note?" She wanted to know.

"This really isn't about the note anymore, P. It's the fact that now I know I can't trust you." I told her. "And I don't know if I want to do that again."

"Why are you so angry about that stupid note?" She asked. "It's almost like—I've been trying to show you that I like you! Ever since the first day I met you. Why can't you see that?"

I shook my head and blinked at her. "P, I don't have feelings for you."

She caught my cheeks between her palms and kissed me. I pushed her away and surged to my feet.

"Stay away from me." I told her.

"Don't you see?" She asked.

Bank rushed to my side.

"I love you." She screeched.

Bank shook his head and led me away from her. Gift fell sobbing but I didn't stop to focus on her.

I was too busy trying to get her taste off my lips but failed until Bank took pity on me and handed me a stick of gum.

I knew then no one could kiss me like Storm—when he kissed me, I wanted more. I wanted to get naked for him and let him do whatever he wanted to me.

With Gift, all I felt was disgust and anger.

Getting through filming was rough. Seua stopped for a few minutes to give me a moment to breathe. Storm left the room to use the bathroom but when he came back, he was angry. Before I could speak, he held out his phone to me—someone had posted a picture of Gift kissing me.

"Storm…"

"No." He shook his head and walked away from me.

When I looked over at Gift, she was smiling, and I knew she had something to do with the posting of that picture. Irritated, I stormed over to her, but Gear caught me around the hips and pulled me back.

Seua asked everyone to leave the room except who was involved with what was happening. He dragged his fingers through his hair then faced us.

"Gift, I'm recasting you." Seua spoke simply.

"You can't do that!" Gift screeched.

"I think I just did!" Seua snapped. "What the hell were you thinking!"

"I was thinking he wanted it!" She fired back.

"What did I do to give you that idea?" Wind snapped. "I'm gay, P! Which means you have the wrong equipment!"

Before she could speak, Seua cut her off.

"I finally got Storm and Wind to get along and now you've stuck your vagina in the middle of things and is ruining it." He growled. "My graduation is dependent on this film! This is not a joke for me! So, get your things and get out!"

"Wind?" Gift pleaded stepping toward me.

Storm shifted his body between hers and mine, forcing her to back up.

She ran from the room with her things. When I turned to Storm, he held up his hands and walked over to his things, gathered it all and left.

"Give him some time." Kai told me. "I'll go after him. Gear—"

"I drove today." Gear told him. "I'll be fine."

"I'm going to go." I managed and turned for the door.

"Hey!" Gear called. "Wait a minute! Don't you go running off on your own too. It's late."

"I'm going home." I told him.

"Gear and I will take you." Seua told me.

I sat in the back of his car, feeling numb. The only words I said was to thank them and wandered off toward the front. When I made it back to the room, Storm wasn't there.

I went through the rest of the week, seeing him only during filming and that was once. He only had one scene that entire week as per the schedule.

When he didn't come home Friday, I sat at his desk with a piece of paper and a pen. I wrote him a note and left for home to my mother.

"Okay, my love." My mother set some soup in the center of the table before sitting. "You've been here since last night and no word as to why you're not okay."

I sighed and scooped some soup into her bowl before doing the same to my own. Even after she placed a piece of pork into my bowl along with vegetables, I couldn't find the word to explain to her what had happened. When I finally did, she sighed and lifted a piece of leek into her mouth.

"Jealousy." Mae told me. "One of the oldest reason people fall apart."

"Jealousy?"

"N'Storm is jealous." She explained. "When the green-eyed monster is involved, he can't see anything but the picture of this girl kissing you. It's obvious he cares for you—he wants you and he doesn't want to share. To complicate this even more, he's probably thinking you're not gay."

"Mae, you know I am."

"I'm not the one you need to convince."

I blinked at her.

"Don't just sit there. Go."

I left the table but ran back to hug her then ran out again. Her laughter followed me out the door and up the stairs to my bedroom.

I called Storm.

No answer.

I sent a number of text messages.

Nothing.

My heart sank.

I climbed out my window against the tree outside. Scaling, I sat on a limb and thought back to what my mother said.

I realized him being jealous felt good, but I needed to explain to him that I didn't enjoy what had happened.

My phone rang and I looked down to see Storm's name on the screen. I quickly answered it.

"Hi," Storm said.

"I'm sorry, P." I whispered. "I should have known she was up to something."

"Where are you?"

"I told you—I'm home for the weekend."

"When are you coming back?"

"Sunday night." I replied. "Are you jealous, P?"

"Yes." Storm replied. "I know I haven't asked you to be my boyfriend. And I know kissing you meant nothing to you. But it still kills me seeing someone else that close to you."

"I didn't know she was going to do that."

"Enjoy your time with your mother." Storm told me. "We will talk when you come home."

"P…"

"I promise." Storm told me.

"There are so many things I want to say." I admitted. "So many things I probably shouldn't say to a man who isn't with me—who isn't my boyfriend. But I don't want to hide anything from you. Even if you walk away after I tell you."

"What kind of things?"

"Um…" I rubbed the back of my neck. "Things I want to do to you—that I want you to do to me."

"Wow."

"I told you." I sighed. "It's bad."

Storm laughed softly. "Let's make a deal. When you come home, we'll talk about the whole Gift thing and what we're going to do about her. Then, we'll discuss these things you want to do to me to see how many I'll let you get away with."

I choked.

"Are you okay?" Storm asked.

"Okay, *khrap.*"

We talked a while longer and by the time I crawled back into the bedroom, I felt much better than I had in days. My mother noticed the change, smiled and shook her head. She accepted a kiss from me to her cheek before I crawled into bed.

I dreamed of Storm that night, of his body over mine and his lips on every part of me.

I woke the next morning and couldn't help the happiness I felt.

I whistled while helping my mother make breakfast, then went to the market to pick up some things for my her.

Spending time with my mother made me happy, healed me and soon I was on my way back to school. To my surprise, Storm came to pick me up at the bus station.

I didn't know how I would get from the terminal to the campus. I'd use what little money I had to buy my mother some groceries. Sighing, I gathered my bag and stepped out of the building to find Storm leaning against the side of his car.

He was sexy, dressed in black jeans, a white t-shirt with his sunglasses over his eyes.

He smirked and waved at me.

I ran over to him, and Storm pulled me into a hug. Sighing, I melted into his muscular chest and allowed him to hold onto me for as long as he wanted. He then picked up my bag and dropped it onto the backseat.

"Hungry?" He asked.

"Yes." I stared at him.

"For food, Wind." Storm dropped his voice sexily.

I blushed and instead of saying anything, I climbed into the passenger side of his car.

Storm hopped in beside me and we drove to a nearby noodle place where he parked, and we took seats close to the actual building on the patio.

"You do know I'm not into women, right?" I asked Storm as he twirled noodles around his chopsticks.

He stopped and looked over at me.

"I'm serious."

"I know."

"Then why were you so jealous of what happened?" I asked.

"I don't know." He admitted. "I saw her with you, and I saw red. One day, I'm going to ask you to be my boyfriend. I know that. I just—right now, I'm not ready. I have some growing up to do."

"And who says I want to be your boyfriend?" I asked, avoiding his eyes.

"I guess we'll just have to wait and see." Storm laughed. "How's your mother?"

"Tired."

Storm

At the end of our Muay Thai session, I peeled off the gloves and picked up a towel and a bottle of water. Gear did the same and we walked out the back of the gym to sit on the edge of the porch, staring down at the greenery below us. This part of the property always made me feel peaceful and whole. After I drank half the contents of my bottle, I exhaled.

"I like boys." I confessed.

"Um—I kind of figured that one out when you almost took Gift's head off for kissing Wind." Gear relied. "As a matter of fact, I've suspected for a while."

"Really?" I asked. "Why didn't you say something?"

"It wasn't my closet to climb out of." Gear shrugged. "Besides, I had my own closet I needed to get out of."

"Who knows?"

"Papa." Gear told me. "I told him two years ago. "I had to figure out how to tell you."

"How did you know for sure that it wasn't just a phase you were going through?"

"Well." Gear set his bottle by his ass.

But it didn't seem as if he was going to say anything else.

I frowned. "Seriously?"

"Seriously, what?" Gear asked.

"You were going to say something, and you stopped."

"I kissed a girl, felt nothing." Gear shrugged. "I kissed a second and a third girl—still nothing. I kissed a boy and liked it—so much so that when I kissed a second and a third boy, it only got better."

We sat like that for a while longer, talking, enjoying the breeze floating upward to the gym and to dance over our skin. Eventually, we reported to the showers, then I drove us back to his place.

"Maybe now that you and Wind are in a good place, you should suggest moving out of the dorms." Gear suggested.

"Wind can't." I told him. "It's one of the rules. Because of his scholarship, he has to remain on campus. And that's only one of the problems."

"Okay—what else could there be, P?"

"Wind is proud." I answered. "He won't be okay with moving into a place where I paid all the bills. Trust me, he's good."

Gear laughed, kissed my head and grabbed his bag to climb from the car. "You get some sleep tonight."

"*Khrap.*"

The entire journey back to the dorms was spent thinking about what I would do with Gift. I was pretty sure she would not just go away. In fact, getting kicked off the set must have come as a blow to her. It was her only way to have access to Wind. If she as in fact obsessed, she'd find something else—most likely something dangerous.

The thought of Wind being in danger angered me. I wanted to put a call in to my father.

Then again, one of the reasons he put me together with Kai when we were children was because he knew Kai would protect me.

No, this was my lover which meant it was my duty to protect him.

With that thought firmly in mind, I parked and made my way across the parking lot. An uneasy feeling filled my insides, but I didn't stop until I was inside the door. I turned and looked out the glass to the dimly lit parking lot and knew something was different.

There had been more lights.

Since I was fine, I made my way up to our room, locked the door behind me, set my bag on the floor and climbed into bed behind Wind. When I snaked my arm around him, he moaned and shimmied back into my chest.

"You're late." He groaned.

"After Muay Thai I spent some time talking to Gear." I replied. "There were a few things he and I needed to hash out."

"Did you two have a fight?" Wind rolled over in the circle of my arm, so my face fell against his neck.

"No." I lifted my head. "We had a very nice talk. Can you just let me hold you for a bit?"

Wind said nothing. He rolled all the way over to face me. He rested his palm to my cheek and kissed me gently.

As he pulled back, I drew him closer to me and kissed him deeper, longer.

"I needed that." I admitted. "One more kiss then I'll let you sleep."

"Stay?"

"I'm staying." I laughed around a playful smooch. "I live here, remember?"

"No. That's not what I meant." His voice cracked. "Stay with me—here—in this bed."

"Oh." I stared into his gaze and knew I was in serious trouble. It seemed I couldn't say no to him, deny him anything. I agreed with a deep kiss that turned into him trying to peel my clothes off my body.

Rolling him to his back, I rose over him, holding his wrists against the bed.

"No." It killed me to say. "We're going to move slow. I'm going to figure out what I want from this relationship, from you. You'll do the same. Once we're both sure, I'll let this happen."

Wind groaned in frustration, pushing his hips upward to show me what was happening to his body.

He was hard, ready.

I kissed him deeply and rolled off him but gathered him into my arms.

I snaked a hand between our bodies as our tongues tangled with each other. Inside his pajamas I wrapped my finger around the source of his discomfort and stroke him in a tight fist.

Wind gasped. "What are you—oh!"

"You've never had a man do this to you?" He asked. "Touch you like this?"

"I haven't even—oh, P—I haven't even done it to myself!"

Smiling, proud to be his first, I took his lips again, all the while stroking him, feeling his body tremble, and hearing the soft sounds he made because of me.

They made my body come alive because I knew I caused them in him.

I knew I made him tremble and whisper my name against my tongue.

"Storm!" He gasped.

His body fell apart for me. Wind pressed his heated cheeks to my neck, panting and sighing. I released him and kissed the side of his head until he was breathing normally again.

"Don't be shy or ashamed." I told him. "What we've done is normal."

"I can't help being shy."

"Was that really your first orgasm, Wind?"

He nodded against me then lifted his head.

"Come take a shower with me." I told him as I scooted out of the bed.

"My knees are weak."

I laughed softly and scooped him up and into my arms. Wind wrapped his arms around me and squealed happily.

The water poured down over us as Wind clung to me, his wet arms tangled around my hips. I kissed the side of his head, holding him close as if in a dance where neither of us wanted to move, afraid the air would come between us.

I caressed his back, loving the smoothness of it with the water gliding over my fingers.

"I need you to be careful when you go about your day."
I finally spoke.

"Why?"

"I don't trust Gift." I advised him. "I don't trust her and
if she hurts you, I'll kill her."

"No need for bloodshed, P." He still hadn't lifted his
head from where it laid on my shoulder. "I'm pretty sure
she gets that I'm not interested by now. I'm not sure what
she thought she could get from me. She knew I wasn't—
well, you know?"

I didn't answer—I merely pulled him closer with one
hand while reaching for the soap with the other.

In silence, I lathered his back, over his ass before
leaving away for him to get is front. I caressed him in
places that had Wind moaning.

I touched him, carefully, softly.

When I rinsed him, he fell heavily against my chest,
panting.

Instead of taking a shower myself, I helped him to dry
off then dressed. Once he was in bed, I went back to finish
my shower, hauled on a pair of shorts and went back to
crawl into bed with him. With the sheets up and over us, I
kissed his neck.

"Go to sleep." I whispered.

"Can I ask—what you did to me earlier—can I do that
to you?"

I trembled. "Yes. But not tonight. Right now, you're
tired and we have a long day ahead of us tomorrow."

Wind sighed, kissed my chin and closed his eyes.

While I waited for the others to arrive for band practice, I video called my grandfather. His face lit up the moment he saw me. He'd always shown me that kind of love but even as an adult, I still couldn't understand it. I never understood how he was able to love my brother and I so completely, so unconditionally when our father rarely spoke to us.

Our father lived in another city and made seeing us a part of the schedule his assistant put together for him. Half the time, he didn't remember and when Gear and I called, he barely had a few words to rub together for us.

After about a year of that kind of attitude, I stopped calling, so did Gear. Our father hardly noticed. We would go months without speaking. Once again, I fell into big brother and father mode for Gear, making sure he was happy, healthy and doing the right things.

Gear won numerous awards for his photography. My father had no idea. He never showed up to any of the award ceremonies and I saw the disappointment in Gear's eyes every time he looked down at me in the audience and I shook my head.

Grandfather, or Papa as we'd taken to calling him, was the splitting image of my father, only less cold and smiled more. I smiled and waved.

"*Sawatdii khrap,* Papa." I greeted him.

"*Ja.*" He grinned. "You look very happy."

I blushed. "Papa. How are you?"

"My knee is giving me some trouble. I think it's going to rain." He teased. "But what else is new? It's not as bad as it could be."

I knew that had been an ongoing issue ever since I was a kid. He'd been in a car accident bringing us home from a day out.

Grandmother passed in it and the rest of us survived. For a long time, he felt bad. He went through a lot—having to learn how to walk again. But now, mostly when the weather is bad, he needed a cane to make it around.

"Have you spoken to your father?" Papa asked.

"No." I replied. "He must be busy."

"That is no excuse." Papa frowned. "He is a father. I've always told him that money comes and goes but his children are very important."

"Papa, Gear and I are okay-khrap." I managed a smile.

It would be nice to have our father be interested in our successes and failures. It would be nice to have him there, being involved, shaping us to be men. But we'd grown to accept what our reality truly was.

Papa winced and massaged his right knee.

"Do you want us to come home?" I asked him. "We could help you with the stairs and the moving around."

"It's only a little pain." He replied.

"Have you given any further thoughts to moving?"

"I lived with your mama here." He told me. "I still feel her here. I don't want to move. If anything, you and your brother can turn one of the rooms on the lower floor into a bedroom for me. When the pain is bad, I could sleep there."

"That's a great idea!" I perked up. "I'll tell Gear and we'll make that happen."

He nodded his agreement. "Tell me, how are you making out with Wind?"

"That's actually why I'm calling." I admitted, the air around me growing serious and almost grim. "Papa, there's something I need to tell you."

"I feel like I should sit down for this." He laughed.

"Um—you're probably right."

I waited until he gritted his teeth and sat in his favourite chair before I spoke again.

142

"Well, you know how I wanted to make things right with Wind?" I asked.

He nodded.

"At some point along the way, I developed—well, feelings for him."

"You're telling me you like boys," Papa said.

"Yes."

"Okay—that makes more sense."

"Aren't you disappointed?" I asked.

"Disappointed?" Papa laughed then sighed.

"Yes, that I don't like girls." I replied. "Isn't that the normal thing for me?"

"Normal is boring." Papa shrugged.

I cleared my throat and rubbed my eyes. "I-I don't—"

"This would be a better conversation if we could do it in person. But Storm, you've always been a little different. You've been entirely too serious for your age, and you always had this *thing* behind your eyes that I couldn't decipher. I didn't know what it was—but as long as you were okay."

"I struggled with it." I sighed. "It wasn't that I didn't want to tell you. It was something I thought was wrong with me."

"Storm, there is nothing wrong with you." Papa shifted. "I believe you should be with the person you love. That makes your life easier, and it makes you happy. If you force it with someone else, eventually, the two of you will grow to hate each other. Then any children you have will suffer. I may be an old man, and not up on the latest trends, but I know happiness. Marriage without love, is no happiness."

"Marriage and children?" I blushed. "Papa."

He laughed softly.

The others showed up and I handed the phone over to my brother so he could say hello to Papa.

I quickly hugged my friends then proceeded to sit around talking to them about our schedule.

We didn't have much planned due to school and the film, but the things we did have coming up paid us well.

"I know you guys are doing this for me." Seua told us.

"Doing what?" Kai asked.

"The hotel—the others." Seua pointed out.

"So?" I asked. "You are family. We aren't doing for you anything you wouldn't do for us."

"That is true." Seua told us. "Thank you."

I bounced Seua with my shoulder and smiled.

"We're having fun." I added. "And since you won't let us help you, we figured if you earned it—you wouldn't feel bad."

Seua rested his head on my shoulder, and we continued with the meeting. When we finally got to the music, it felt as if the weight of world was off my shoulders. We had fun with it, switching our setlist around, updating a few of the older songs.

By the end of the rehearsals, I was relaxed.

Gear left to meet with a few of his friends, and I sat around wanting to tell Kai and Seua what I'd told my grandfather. They were surprised. Afterall, they thought I was in fact bisexual. I thought about it then shook my head.

"Nope." I smiled. "Boys only."

Kai laughed. "Well, now you can go after N'Wind without worrying."

"What?" I asked.

"We've seen the way you kiss him on set." Seua wrung the cap off his water. "You can't make that up. It's not the kiss, really. It's the way you hold him, like you're afraid he'll break. Then you look at him with this intensity, like the rest of us don't exist in the room."

"Seua is right." Kai told me. "It looks good on you."

"Wind is still gun-shy." I explained. "Maybe it's because of his father—I don't know. I guess I just need to be patient. I really feel something strong for him."

"Then use that." Seua told me. "Use that as the foundation to build on."

144

Later, as I left the building, I noticed something strange.

There was a white chalk mark on one of the back tires of my car.

I knew immediately someone wanted to keep track of whether or not my car had moved.

Glancing around, I checked the backseat, then slipped to my knees to look under. After checking the wheel wells, I drove the car home.

I said nothing to Wind, since I didn't want him to worry, but I sent a text message to Kai while Wind was in the shower.

"*Contact Dew and have him switch my car out.*" I sent.

"*Model?*"

I thought about it for a moment then shrugged and replied. "*The newest Lexus LC in all black. I need it here by lunch tomorrow.*"

"*And the Bentley?*"

"*Have it taken to Gear's beach house and park it in the back garage.*" I paused to think over what I was telling my friend to do. "*I'll figure out what to do with it later.*"

"*What's going on, Storm?*" Kai asked. "*The last time you did this one of your father's enemies was coming after you. Should I be worried?*"

"*I'm not too sure yet. This is precaution for now.*" I looked up toward the bathroom door then back down at my phone knowing Kai was already switching from best friend to bodyguard. "*Try not to worry. I'll let you know if anything changes.*"

"You're so serious." Wind's voice caught my attention. "Everything okay?"

I deactivated the screen to my phone and set it on my desk. Although I hadn't asked him to be mine, it was still my duty to protect him. It was still my duty to ensure he was happy and that he wasn't distracted from his schooling and what made him happy.

Instead of telling him my suspicions, I smiled. "Okay-*khrap.*"

My father had made some enemies over the years, and while he'd made the last person who came after his family suffer—horribly, it could be happening again.

Feeling the weight of the Bannarasee name weighing me down, I took Wind's hand and pulled him into my arms.

"P?" He questioned.

"It's been a long day." I confided. "A test, other classes, band practice, it feels like a lot."

Wind hugged me back, his arms tight around me then up to snake his fingers through my hair as he kissed my neck. "What can I do?"

"You're doing it."

I sighed, gave in to him. I relinquished my need for control.

Having Wind hold me soothed me in a way that was out of this world. It was as if he his arms was the medicine I needed all day, all my life.

"The last time I was home, my mother seemed overly tired," Wind said, pulling from my arms to sit beside me. "I wanted to go home this weekend, make sure she rests while I take care of her. Um—if you're not busy, would you like to come? Fresh air, a change of pace—it could be good for you."

My heart soared happily. "Are you sure? Especially with—"

"My mother knows I like boys." Wind looked down at his hands. "Unless you don't want her to know."

"Why wouldn't I want her to know?" I took his hands in mine and lifted the back of them to my lips. "I already told you what my goal is—to be yours. Right now, I don't think I deserve you but I'm working to."

"P…I'm not that big of a catch." Wind explained. "I have no money. I barely have an education—I don't think my family name means much to anyone but me. I bring nothing to this relationship."

"Don't ever say that." I pushed. "I have enough money for the both of us. And it may make me sound like an ass to say this, but I learned from you that money isn't everything. You bring more to this relationship than I do. You bring you."

Wind blushed but didn't look away. Instead, he framed the left side of my cheek. "Can I kiss you?"

"Any time you want."

Wind smiled and pushed forward to kiss me. It was soft at first, until he wrapped his free hand around my back and deepened the kiss.

My control slowly slipped away but I didn't stop kissing him until I groaned softly.

"Are you in?" Wind asked."

"I will need to buy her a gift." I managed around the daze in my head.

"I'm sure my mother doesn't need a gift."

I shrugged. "I can't just show up to meet her with nothing. It's rude. Maybe her favourite chocolates. Or wine, does she drink wine? Maybe that's too telling. What about a nice scarf? She could use it when the weather gets cold—women like scarves, right?"

Wind kissed me quickly. I knew it was because I was rambling, my nerves showing.

When I looked at him, Wind smiled. "You can buy her beautiful roses. She loves them—that would make her smile."

"Roses? That's it?"

Wind nodded. "That's it. When we just moved to the village, there was an old man who lived close to the entrance. He had these beautiful roses."

He paused as the memories made a tear rolled down his cheek. I reached forward to use my thumb to wipe it away.

"I had no money—he realized that I could read English. So, had me translate some letters for him in return for five roses."

"You're a wonderful son."

Wind smiled through his tears. "I didn't know if she would like them. But she told me a story of when she was a little girl and would help her mother in her rose garden."

"So, they are her favourite?"

Wind nodded.

I inhaled deeply through my nose, held it for a moment then exhaled it through my mouth. "Let's go meet Mae."

"Don't call her that." Wind pouted. "You're not my boyfriend."

"Not yet."

Wind groaned. "I've been thinking." He turned, climbed over me and sat on my lap.

"About?"

"You'll see." Wind sighed, pushing me backward onto the bed.

I knew what he'd been thinking about when Wind reached down and grabbed me. My eyes widened and I held my breath.

"Wind, only if you're sure."

"I don't want to be a selfish lover." Wind gasped, grinding his hips down against mine. "You've been so— harder."

Pressing my palms to the small of Wind's back, I pushed downward, causing Wind to ride against me a lot more intimately than I'd been with anyone else.

Wind eased back and reached down to pull my pants and boxers down. I pushed to my elbows to watch him.

Wind stared down at me, his eyes wide, his cheeks pink. For some reason, having him look at me like that made me shy. I tried pulling him off me, but Wind locked his knees at the sides of mine and wrapped his fingers around me and squeezed.

I whimpered his name and couldn't stop my hips from rolling up ward, driving my hardness through his fist and shuddering at how good it felt.

"It's been so long." I confessed. "Tightened your fist…"

I came for Wind, my entire body trembling as I moaned for him. Wind leant over me and kissed my lips, my shoulders, my forehead and nose. His actions soothed me and all I could do was pull him into the circle of my arms and clung to him.

cling

Wind

Storm met me with a bunch of the most perfect roses I'd ever seen. He wanted to drive but I had to explain to him that his fancy car wouldn't survive the drive into the village.

We bussed the first half. When the bus stopped for us to use the bathroom and get snacks, Storm hurried ahead to use the bathroom and when I joined him again, he had two bags with food and drinks for us.

We ate together, sharing everything then talked about everything and nothing at the same time.

At some point, while sharing his music, I rested my head on his shoulder and fell asleep. When I woke again, he was asleep as well, his fingers laced with mine.

Smiling, I lifted the back of his hand to my lips, placed a kiss there, then lowered it back to my lap. Being careful not to wake him, I stared out the window, watching trees fly by the bus, unable to quell the happiness to rise inside me.

Once we arrived at the end of the first half of the trip, we waited a few minutes for my mother's best friend's son to pick us up.

He tried getting me to sit beside him in the front, but I declined and sat in the back with Storm.

I watched Storm carefully for any sign of regret. But he was too busy staring out the window at the trees.

"It's not too late to turn back." I told him.

"Yes, it is." Storm smiled at me then returned his gaze out the window. "And now, I don't want to turn back."

"Your mother says you're studying business." The young man behind the wheel spoke.

"Um—mm." I replied.

"Do you like it?" He asked.

"I do."

"I have a few more months to decide what I want to do." The driver continued. "I'm not sure yet, though."

I said nothing to that. Instead, I turned my attention out my window, still amazed by the far and thatched houses as we zoomed by from time to time.

"Do you have a lover?" The driver blurted out.

"Yes." I replied when I got over the shock.

"You do?" He wanted to know. "Who?"

"I am." Storm told him.

My cheeks flushed as Storm reached over to take my hand as if to stress his point.

The driver fell into silence then and I watched the tense way Storm's jawline was set.

Each time I looked up, the young man was glancing back through the mirror. Shaking my head, I clung to Storm's hand for the rest of the ride.

By the time we wound up in front of Mae's place, our driver was bad tempered and huffy.

He couldn't have liked me. My mother met his mother at the hotel and he and I didn't grow up together. Mae used to talk about him, saying his father died leaving the family with nothing. That he'd cheated on the mother, developed a disease that caused him to scream when he peed. I thought it was disgusting and didn't particularly want to know the rest.

"My love!" My mother darted out the house to hug me tightly.

She thanked our driver who merely offered her wai and sped off down the dirt road in a cloud of dust. She started after him then returned her attention to us.

"You must be Storm," she said.

Storm clasped his palms in front of his face and bowed to her. She touched the top of his head then led us into the house.

After Storm offered her the flowers, she sniffed them, giggled then wandered off to put them in the one vase she owned. It was a gift my father gave her on their second date.

When I was younger, I often wondered what kind of man gave a woman a vase on their second date.

Then I realized—It was a man who wanted to give his woman flowers every chance he had.

We weren't rich—Pa brought my mother wide flowers every Saturday morning.

I showed Storm to my bedroom since we didn't have a spare.

"I'm sure it's not what you're used to." I told him. "I'm sorry, but you'll have to share with me."

"No—this is cute." Storm told me. "It's comfortable. Lived in. Something's missing, though."

"Oh?"

"I thought you would have stuffed animals or something." Storm smirked. "Maybe a teddy to cuddle with."

I smacked his arm.

Storm merely laughed.

I picked up one of the pillows from the bed and dropped it on the floor.

Before bed, I'd grab one of the blankets from where my mother kept the clean linens.

"You can take the bed." I told him.

"You're not sleeping on the floor." Storm told me.

"My mother would be down the hall." Wind whispered.

"I'm very sure your mother knows we're together." Storm shrugged. "I may not have experience with a mother—but they know things."

"We're not together." I folded my arms.

I wasn't sure why I was fighting it. The thought of being Storm's boyfriend made me happy. It sent a warm feeling through me that I loved, that made me feel whole. But I felt as if I had to play hard to get, to not make it easy for him. I wanted him not to take me for granted once I finally gave in to his charms.

"What do you think I would do to you tonight, Wind?" Storm asked.

"Nothing." I told him.

It wasn't what I thought he would do to me—it was what I wanted him to do to me that scared me.

"I wouldn't make love to you here, Wind." Storm explained as he walked over to the window to look out. He remained silent until he was standing in front of me again, Storm leaned in to kiss my ear.

"You don't want to?" I asked.

"You know better." Storm's voice was a soft growl.

He nipped at it and that sensation had me gripping the front of his shirt.

I whimpered.

I wanted him to do it again.

"When I make love to you, Wind." He traced the lobe with his tongue. "I want to hear you scream."

"I'm sure you're not that good of a lover." I whimpered.

"No?"

He nipped at my earlobe with his teeth then sucked the hurt away.

I pushed his chest.

"Challenge accepted." Storm smirked.

"That wasn't a challenge."

"You can't question a man's virility and not give him a chance to prove himself." Storm stepped toward me again and kissed my shoulder then the side of my neck.

He backed me across the room until my back hit the dresser.

I groaned.

He gripped the dresser on both sides of me, kissed my throat then across to my shoulder. Storm pressed his body into mine and I could feel just how hard his entire frame was.

I liked it—a lot.

I trembled. "We have to go back to Mae."

Storm caught my arm as I squeezed my body away from his. When I looked up at him, it was in time for his lips to descend on mine.

I sighed, pressed a palm to his chest and melted into him. I gave in to his kiss, fisting the front of his shirt, trying to keep his mouth on mine.

My body reacted to him like it always did and by the time Mae called for us to come and eat something, all I wanted was for Storm to take me to the bed and test just how quiet I could be.

"P?"

"Mm."

Storm hugged me tightly.

"Do you really want to make love to me?" I asked.

"All the time." His voice cracked. "We should go back to Mae."

"But—"

"We can continue later." He helped me fix my hair and we went back down the stairs to sit with my mother to eat.

We ate dinner at the table, talking about our day. I explained to my mother that this weekend she wouldn't lift a finger. She wasn't impressed but I needed to give her a moment to catch her breath since she'd been working so hard of late.

Mae gave in, and Storm and I instantly took over.

We cut her a slice of cake we'd brought from the city, brewed her a cup of tea an sat her on the porch with a book.

Storm and I took to task of doing the dishes and cleaning up the kitchen.

Once we were finished, I seasoned some pork for dinner the next day, stuck it in the fridge in an air-tight container then checked on Mae.

The night was quiet, even after Mae went to sleep. Storm and I showered, one after the other then crawled into bed, lying beside each other. The insects of the night sang their regular songs outside the home as the moon rose int the sky. We could see it, big and round—almost as if it was smiling at me in through the window.

"I've never had a family dinner before." Storm admitted.

"Never?" I asked.

"My parents never—" Storm exhaled. "They were busy. I was raised by the help until my grandfather stepped in. Then we raised Gear as best we could. I'm just—sitting around with a mother to eat a meal felt good."

"What do you mean raised by the help?"

"My father was always working." He told me. "Crime doesn't go on a break because those who uphold the law wants to spend time with their kids. So, no parents to tuck me in, check my homework—that sort of thing."

"What about your mother?"

"Can we not talk about that?" He rolled over to look at me.

I faced him and wiggled my body closer so I could wrap my arms around him. He snuggled into my chest, pressing his face into my throat. I pulled the sheet up to our shoulders and settled with him.

There was a beauty in the way he allowed me to hold him. Most men like Storm wouldn't have been so vulnerable in front of anyone.

Kissing his head, I closed my eyes.

For the first time in a long time, I slept all through the night. When Storm had his nightmares, I held him closer, kissing his forehead, down to the tip of his nose. He cried into my chest, his tears soaking through my shirt.

"Shhh." I hushed him. "I'm here. I'm not letting you go and in my arms, Storm, you're safe."

He settled back into sleep, and I drifted off with him.

Storm woke up to use the bathroom, but other than that, he slept.

I woke up before him the next morning and after making coffee and left it to keep warm, I wandered away from the house, along familiar paths for a walk.

I cut across a couple of fields of neighbours, waving to them as they worked away.

My mother's friend stopped to speak with me. Her son was the young man who'd driven us into the village. She did some small talk, but she was really interested in finding out if I was really seeing someone.

"Mm." I replied.

"Well, young men tend to date others to figure out what they're into." P'Anna told me. "Maybe you should try someone you're familiar with."

"Emotions don't work like that, P." I informed her. "Storm is a good guy—he has feelings for me, and they are mutual."

She nodded and patted my shoulder. P'Anna turned to pick up a bag which she handed to me. I looked in and arched a brow.

"Um?"

"Give this to your mother." She told me. "I knew she wanted to make some red curry."

After offering her wai, I continued my way back toward Mae's place.

I thought about P'Anna's son and Storm. Their differences, their physical similarities and everything that caused me to be attracted to one and not the other.

It wasn't that her son wasn't handsome—he was very good-looking. His body was a little sleeker than Storm's. His dark hair, brown eyes—when he looked at me, however, my skin crawled.

Storm looked at me and I wanted him—he smiled at me and every part of me come to life.

Yes, Storm was the one for me.

At the house, I stood outside and looked up.

It was still quiet.

After checking on Mae and Storm, I grabbed a bag and wandered away from the house again to the local grocery. I picked up the rest of the recipe for red curry, some milk and sweets.

This time, when I made it back, Mae was sitting in the kitchen, sipping coffee and in deep conversation with Storm.

Mae was the first to see me as I stepped in, and she cheered.

"You're back."

I nodded. "Mae, P'Ann gave me some bamboo sprouts for red curry. I'll make some tonight and leave it for you, so you don't have to cook for a few days."

"Aww, thank you, my love." She replied and sipped from her tea.

I walked up behind Storm and settled for a gentle touch to his shoulder, though what I craved was a kiss.

"I'm going to spend some time with P'Ann after breakfast." Mae told us. "I want to give you two some time alone."

"Mae!" I blushed.

"Do you think I don't know the two of you are together?" She laughed. "I'm your mother. I can read your mind, Wind."

I pressed my face to Storm's shoulder.

He only laughed and kissed my head.

"You don't have to leave, Mae." He told her.

My mom giggled. I could tell she liked Storm.

"I want the walk." She told us. "And since you two won't let me do any work, I figured visiting a friend is a nice thing."

"Mae, really." I tried convincing her to stay.

In the end, she wound up leaving Storm and I together. We cleaned up, then carried fruits into the backyard where we sat together talking about the film we were almost finished making.

My cell rang, interrupting the peace and I arched a brow and picked it up.

"Wind," Bank greeted me. "I went to the dorms but you're not there. Wanted to see if you want to go out tonight."

"Um—I'm actually at my mother's." I told him. "You have very bad timing."

Bank laughed. "I hear P'Storm isn't around. Am I to assume he's with you?"

"Yes. Why?" I looked over at Storm who had his head tilted back and his eyes closed.

"No reason." Bank said mischievously. "You took him home to meet Mae already. You two must be serious."

I groaned.

"What's the matter?" Storm asked.

"Nothing. It's Bank." I replied. "He's being all weird."

"I'm not being weird. Let me talk to him."

Against, my better judgement, I placed Bank on speaker phone.

"Bank?" Storm called.

"P!" Bank cheered. "How is Mae liking her son-in-law?"

"What?" I cried. "Goodbye, Bank!"

"Awww!" Bank protested.

I hung up but Storm couldn't stop smiling.

Shaking my head, I allowed him to pull me into his arms as he laughed out loud and kissed my forehead.

We didn't sit around for much longer. Storm wanted to take me up to the bedroom, but I managed to talk him into going to the market.

There, I saw a side of him I didn't think many others saw. Aside from a couple of phone calls from Kai and Seua then Gear, Storm put away his phone and had fun with me.

Eating food from roadside sellers, playing games at a pop-up carnival and buying small trinkets, he laughed, back hugged me, tried finding a cute nickname for me then giggled when I frowned at him.

He was radiant, funny, animated—my heart opened even more to him without him even trying.

The weekend was a success.

Mae fell for Storm almost as hard as I had. She'd began calling him her son, and Storm didn't correct her. Though I grumbled out loud, I secretly enjoyed the way they interacted with each other.

I love that he wandered from the house to pick her wildflowers before our ride arrived.

His jealousy caused him to hire a driver to pick us up in the village. rather than using P'Ann's son again. My mother laughed and shook her head when she realized what Storm had done while I tried getting him to cancel the ride.

"You don't trust me." I eyed him.

"That's not it." Storm replied.

"Then why?"

"Jealousy." He told me after a shrug. "I don't like him hitting on you."

"He wasn't hitting on me." I pleaded. "He asked if I was seeing anyone."

"If you'd said no, he would have started chasing you."

"If I wasn't seeing anyone." I pointed out.

My mother had opened a bag of chips at this point and was looking back and forth between us as we carried on.

"So, you want him to hit on you?" Storm demanded.

"That's not what I was say—"

A loud horn caught our attention from outside.

"Mae," Storm said as he hugged her.

"It was good meeting you, Storm." Mae told him. "You take care of yourself, okay?"

Storm stood back to look into her eyes, nodded and hugged her again.

Once he released her, I got in there to hug her as well. She murmured her love for me and hugged me a little harder.

Outside, Storm hugged my mother again and I knew why.

His mother hadn't cared.

Mae had taken him in, gave him experiences as a family that he never had with his own.

Storm was happy.

For the longest time, after we climbed into the back of the chauffeured car, I stared at him.

"You're staring." Storm's voice was soft.

"I am." I replied unashamedly.

He looked at me.

"When are you going to ask me to be your boyfriend?" I asked him.

"I don't know."

"You don't know?"

He touched my cheek then tapped my nose gently. "But I'll only have you."

"I can't have you be with anyone else."

"Then tell me."

"I don't want you with anyone else."

Storm smiled and kissed the right corner of my lips then the left.

"I promise." He kissed my forehead. "My body is only yours for as long as you want it."

My heart soared happily and though we were in public, I cuddled into his side. Storm wrapped his arms around my shoulder and rested his head on top of mine.

Going back to school meant band practice, filming, classes and a whole slew of other headaches that came with a reintroduction to reality.

Though Storm and I lived together, I saw him in the mornings, at nights, and if we're lucky, we were able to sneak away for a little time at lunch.

We weren't sure how it happened, but it had gotten out that Storm and I were dating. Though no one was really bothering me about it, each time I entered the room, I knew they were speaking about me.

In our English class, Bank fell into the chair beside me and glanced around. When he caught a few girls staring he sighed.

"Can I help you?" He asked.

They quickly shuffled to turn away.

"What's going on?" I asked him.

"They are trying to confirm if you and Storm are really dating." Bank replied in a soft voice. "They don't believe that Storm would date you as they know you aren't wealthy."

My heart sank.

Bank rubbed my shoulder. "Don't worry about them. Storm, you and I know this is about more than money."

"Still, are you sure you want to sit with me? They might start talking about you too."

"I don't mind them talking." Bank reached into his bag for his books and dropped them unnecessarily loud on his desk. "Let them."

We went through class then gathered our things and walked together from the building.

All along the way people were whispering and staring. Bank draped an arm around my shoulder, and I was pretty sure those pictures would pop up on Storm's phone and all the little secret group within seconds.

The attention made me sick to my stomach, I rushed into the bathroom and threw up.

Bank walked me to filming, handed me a snack bar and a bottle of water. "Here."

"*Khob kun.*" I thanked him.

I was peeling open the wrapper of the bar when the door opened, and Kai stepped out.

He smiled when he saw us and waved. After he headed down the hall, I gave Bank one more helpless look before leaving him to enter the room we would be using to film.

Bank sent me a text message the moment the door closed. "*If P'Storm can't walk with you, call me.*"

"*I'm not a baby. I can take care of myself.*" I sent the reply hastily.

"*That's not the point.*"

I didn't have time to reply to that. One of the makeup girls was already dragging me toward the section of the space put aside for me to get ready. I looked around and found Storm in conversation with one of the other cast members. They were pointing up to the rafters and laughing.

When he finally noticed me staring, he walked away from the guy he'd been speaking to and hunched down in front of me.

"Hi." He greeted me, concern filling his gaze.

"I'm fine." I lied.

"Could you give us a second?" Storm asked her.

She nodded and walked off and Storm stood and pulled me to my feet. He hugged me and suddenly, I was home.

"I know what happened today." He told me. "I'm sorry."

"Don't be. I expected some backlash." I admitted, peeling myself from his embrace. "I just didn't think they'd be calling me unworthy. They don't mind that you're with a guy. They mind that it's me."

Storm rubbed his eyes. "I didn't know we cared what others thinks."

"Usually, no. But what if they're right?"

"They're not right."

"How do you know?" I asked.

"Because they aren't the ones dating you." He growled. "They aren't the ones who feel as if they can't breathe without you—why should what they think matter?"

"Because they have the power to make you miserable."

"Then they obviously don't know what I'm capable of." Storm grumbled.

For the first time since I'd known him, I was afraid of Storm. There was something fierce in his eyes, something that flashed like lightening that sent a strange tremor through me. That one look told me that Storm could be loving and soft. But that he was also capable of some very dark things.

"P…just—"

"I'm not letting you go." Storm told me determinedly. "I'm not letting you go—don't ask me to."

"I'm just saying maybe we should take a break and let this breathe."

Storm grunted but didn't have a chance to speak as Seua entered the room and called things to order.

"You're giving up on me." Storm nodded, the hurt in his eyes palpable.

"I'm not a coward."

"Yes, you are." Storm's voice hitched.

He walked away, and I fell back into my chair on the brink of tears.

I blinked them back—I didn't want to have the make-up artist start all over because my life was in shambles.

At the end of filming, I would usually wait for Storm. We'd stop for a nice cold drink at a late-night shop a little out of our way to the dorms, sat on the sidewalk to drink and talk and if we were alone, a few stolen kisses.

Those were some of the best times of my life.

Storm would proudly take selfies of us and post on social media without caption, leaving his followers guessing.

Most of them gushed about how cute of couple we would make. A few of them weren't happy that their idol could possibly be going off the market. They even went as far as to say I wasn't cute, and that Storm could do better.

Those weren't the ones that bothered me.

The ones that bothered me were the ones at my school who whispered and gossiped and said I wasn't worthy.

At the end of filming, I couldn't deal with a detour to the dorms. I couldn't seem to reconcile my need to love him with my need to protect him from the eyes of the world and people's tongues.

While he was still filming, I gathered my things and snuck out a side door that led me across the parking lot and around the side of the building.

I was nearing the front of the building when something heavy crashed against the back of my head. I looked down in time to see the earth moving up to meet my face.

Then—

Nothing.

No, then there was darkness.

Storm

I spent the night looking for Wind. It wasn't like him to not come home. By the time daybreak happened, I was looking through my contacts to find his mother's phone number when my phone rang, and Bank's name popped up on it.

"Bank, is Wind with you?" I asked by way of greeting.

"Kind, P." He replied. "That's why I'm calling."

My heart simply stopped as I waited for him to tell me what news he had. When he did, I hung up the phone, grabbed my keys and bolted from the doors. I sped from the parking lot, almost running over a group of girls who were walking entirely too slow across the screen then jumped the curve leaving the lot.

At the hospital, I tore through the halls, found out where Wind was and was greeted by Bank who tried speaking to me.

"Where is he?" I asked.

"I'll take you to him but calm down." Bank told me. "If somehow he's awake, you can't go in there angry. He can't see you like this."

Broken, I held my breath and rested my forehead to his shoulders, trying to scrape myself together.

Bank rubbed my back.

When I stood up again, Bank nodded and pointed toward the room where Wind was.

It took everything in me not to run into the room screaming his name.

My knees trembled with each step. But I made my way in and looked down into his face.

He seemed so still.

His right eye was swollen shut. His face was covered in scrapes and bruises.

"He's sleeping off the pain meds." Bank explained. "I told the doctors he was my brother so they would let me stay with him or tell me anything."

"What happened?" I leaned over to kiss his forehead, to drag my lips down to his nose.

"I don't know, P." Bank replied. "A friend of mine found him unconscious, knew we were friends and called me. I had him bring Wind here."

I caressed Wind's cheek. "I'm going to find out who did this."

"What can I do?"

"You're doing it." I wanted to turn to Bank but I couldn't take my eyes off Wind's face. "I promised to protect him. How could I not have protected him from this?"

"Because you can't be in two places at once." Bank rested a hand on my shoulder. "Because no matter how much you want to, you can't protect him from everything."

I sighed.

"I tried getting the video footage from the entrance." Bank explained. "But they wouldn't release it to me."

"Give me the info." I told Bank.

Once he did, I sent it off to Kai.

It didn't take long for Kait to get the information we needed and called back. Bank agreed to go with Kai to find the guys who attacked Wind.

Alone with Wind, I climbed into bed with him, and cuddled into his side.

I tried sleeping, to get some rest for the next morning. But no matter what I did, I couldn't sleep. The thought of someone coming in to attack him again sat on my head, threatening to weigh me down.

A nurse came in to check on him and I almost broke his arm.

"Sorry." I apologized. "Knee-jerk reaction."

The nurse shook his head, checked on Wind and left us again. I was standing by the window when I thought I heard Wind calling my name.

"P'Storm?"

Turning, he was sitting up in bed. I rushed over to kneel by his side and to frame his face with both palms.

"Hi." My voice cracked. "Hi."

"I'm sorry." He sobbed.

Rising to sit by his side, I scooped him into my arms and held onto him. "Shh."

"I wanted some time to think." He admitted. "I didn't think this would happen."

"Rest." I advised him. "I'm going to find out what happened. For now, I'm going to take care of you."

We didn't have much alone time together.

I was leaning in for a kiss when Seua, Gear and the rest of the film's cast descended on the room. I kept getting pushed further and further away from the bed until I found myself outside the room looking in, listening to their concern for him.

I sighed.

It made no sense fighting it.

They liked Wind and I couldn't be angry at that.

Still a little frustrated, I wandered down the hall to a quieter spot and began making calls. In the end, I went back to the room and sat on the side of the bed to kiss Wind deeply.

The others giggled and cheered.

"I have to go for a bit." I told him. "Gear and Seua will stay with him. How about I bring you back a burger?"

"Yes, please." Wind replied. "P'Storm?"

"Mm?"

He crooked his finger, motioning for me to come closer. When I did, he pulled me down for a kiss.

It stunned me at first—since the others were still with us. But I moaned and returned the kiss.

"Come back soon, na?" Wind told me.

I nodded, unable to stop the smile that seemed permanently glued to my lips. "Mm."

When he winked at me, I took Seua aside and asked him to stay with Wind until I returned.

"Of course."

Leaving the hospital, I couldn't stop the anger that had been fighting to push to the surface when I saw the bruises on Wind's face. My anger rose to the surface and by the time I climbed into my car, it was almost blinding.

When I arrived at the warehouse, I parked beside Kai's motorcycle and made my way inside. I rolled up my sleeves as I went before stopping to greet Kai outside a door.

"Apparently, he's not afraid of me." Kai smiled.

"You only found one?"

Kai nodded. "The other is in hiding. I think this one knows where but he's not talking."

"Where's Bank?" I asked.

"He went back to his place to finish an assignment that's due tomorrow," Kai said. "He's also digging for the other guy's hiding place."

Exhausted and at the length of my rope, I let myself into the room and hunched down in front of the guy who seemed to be sleeping. I slapped him against one cheek then the other.

"Wake up."

He gasped and as if he didn't remember where he was, he tried struggling against the ropes Kai had used to restrain him.

"Sorry to disturb your slumber." I growled lowly. "But I have questions."

The man glared at me.

I ignored his stare, pulled out my phone, called up a picture of Wind and thrust it in his face.

"Do you remember him?" I asked. "You should because he's going to be the reason I cut out your tongue."

He trembled but kept his head up.

"I need to know why you attacked him." I pushed.

"I'm not talking."

"No?" I put the phone away then grabbed him by the throat.

I ensure I squeezed until he began sputtering, struggling for breath.

"Do you want to reconsider?" I asked him, digging my thumb into the flesh of his throat.

Nothing.

"Do you know who I am?" I stood, leaning in so he could get a good look. "Think about it."

I took some of the pressure off, but still held onto him. The moment he recognized me, I saw the fear fill his gaze like storm clouds slowly drifting across the sky to block out the sun.

"You're *his* son." The young man squeaked.

"Let me ask you again—"

"It was her!" The man managed as I released his throat. "She paid us to do it!"

"Who?"

"We don't deal with names." He replied. "But I have a picture in my phone, in my pocket."

I rummaged through his pockets for his phone and released him so he could scroll to the picture he was referring to. When I saw who it was, I handed the phone to Kai then back to the shaking guy in front of me.

"Please don't tell your father." He pleaded.

"I won't tell my father." I promised him. "You'll have to deal with my wrath. And trust me, you're not going to like it over here either."

When he yelped, I knocked him out with a fist and restrained him again to the chair.

"What are you going to do to him?"

"Have him taken to the tower." I dusted off my sleeve. "Bury him up to his neck. If he can get himself out, then he deserves to live. If not, it is what it is."

Kai nodded. "What about her?"

"I want her dead." I told him. "But for the moment, have one of the guys keep an eye on her. I'm not ready to deal with her yet. I'm taking Wind home so he can get some rest."

With his instructions, Kai and I bumped fists and I left to head back to the hospital. As promised, I stopped at Gear's favorite burger joint and bought enough food for all of us. Before going back to the room, I found a bathroom and cleaned myself up.

At his room, Wind was lying in the bed, snacking on some jelly with Gear fast asleep beside him.

"Shh." Wind pressed a finger to his lips. "He's exhausted."

Nodding, I kissed both their foreheads then pulled up the extra chair.

"I brought you food." I held up the bag. "It's from Gear's favourite place."

"It smells good." Wind replied. "The doctor says I can go home later today."

"Good." I was busy handing out food and drinks. "I want to take you home."

Wind looked at me and smirked.

"Don't be naughty." I told him.

Seua choked. "Would you two wait until you're alone. There is a child in the room."

"Where?" I looked around.

"I meant Gear." Seua laughed.

I laughed softly.

"I was editing the song with the intro to the movie." Seua bit into his burger.

He then set the laptop on the foot of the bed and hit play.

"Tell me what you think," he said.

We watched it and I nodded. "That is so good."

"I love it." Wind squealed. "I'm in a movie!"

We laughed and that woke Gear up.

We ate, talked for a while until the doctor released Wind to go home. Seua and Gear left together, and I helped Wind into my car and drove him back toward the dorms. He talked me into stopping for ice cream but the moment we arrived at our room, I helped him into bed.

I cuddled him in silence.

"You're going after them," Wind said.

"Yes."

It didn't make sense lying to him.

"This could be dangerous, P." Wind pointed out. "I don't want you getting hurt because of me."

"I'll be okay." I dragged my lips long his hairline. "I need to do this."

"Why do you need to do this?"

"Because I should have protected you." I answered. "And since I wasn't able to do that, I'm going to make them suffer."

"P…"

I said nothing.

"I shouldn't have left."

"This isn't your fault." I told him softly. "For tonight, we won't talk about it. Later, I'll help you take a shower, then make you some dinner and we'll cuddle more."

Wind sighed, wiggled his body to get more comfortable against me and sighed. I didn't complain—I held onto him, feeling happy he was safe and where he was meant to be.

I tried imagining myself without him and it hurt my heart so badly, I winced.

I pushed his hair from his forehead and placed a kiss against his warm flesh and held him tighter."

"P?" Wind asked. "Are you okay?"

"Be my boyfriend."

Wind pulled away to sit up and look down into my face. "P."

"Be my boyfriend."

When he stared at me, lips trembling, I sat up, faced him, and took his hands in mine.

"I can't lose you, Wind." I confessed.

"But, P, we still have the issue with the rumors and the—"

"I'll figure it out later, but I need you to agree."

Wind hung his head for a while before tossing himself into my chest.

"I agree." He told me.

"You—does this mean you're my boyfriend?"

Wind laughed. "It means you're my boyfriend."

"Fine, we'll compromise. We're both boyfriends."

"That doesn't make any sense." Wind told me. "But sure."

Sitting back, I kissed him as deeply as I could.

It took a few days for Wind's injuries to heal enough so makeup could cover them so we could continue filming. His eye was no longer swollen, and his busted lip was on its way to being healed.

Still, he went to school even though I would have preferred him stay home until he was fully healed.

People stared but I didn't have to worry. Bank had remained by Wind's side through all of it.

When I finally could go to his campus to get him, I found him in the canteen with Bank and a couple others from their English class.

I listened to the chatter around and frowned. I walked through the canteen to where Wind was standing with Bank.

I wrapped my arm around his waist, pulled him into my chest and sniff-kissed his cheeks.

Wind wrapped his arms around my neck, giggled and pressed his forehead to my shoulder.

He was blushing.

I smirked at Bank who shook his head.

The collective gasps around me did nothing for my mood. I didn't care what any of them thought. After dropping a real kiss to the side of Wind's head, I exhaled.

"Are you ready to go?" I asked him.

"We have to stop to by your grandfather a gift." Wind told me. "I can't just show up with my empty hands. Especially if he knows I'm your boyfriend."

I groaned and pouted at him. The truth was, I wanted to get him to my grandfather's so I could get him alone in my room.

Wind smacked my arm. "I know what you're thinking, P'Storm. Stop it."

I laughed while tangling my fingers with his.

We made it back to the dorms and packed while we waited for Gear to pick us up. When he finally arrived and we set out on our way, we had him stop at the local mall, and Wind picked up a gift for Papa.

While Gear grabbed his bag and darted into the house, calling for Papa, Wind seemed to be frozen when he climbed from the car and looked up at the mansion in front of him.

"Um—are you sure I should be here?" Wind asked.

"You're my boyfriend." I took his hand and led him into the house. "Of course, you should be here."

We entered just as Papa was hugging Gear. The two of them turned to look at us. Wind shifted closer to my side and pulled his hand from mine.

Papa hugged me then focused on Wind who offered him wai.

"You must be N'Wind," Papa said. "Come on in, Gear and Storm will get you something to drink then show you to where you're sleeping tonight."

Wind nodded.

While Gear made lemonade, I took Wind's hand and brought him up to my room. Once we were alone, Wind exhaled and collapsed on the large bean bag chair by the window. Putting our bags close to the bed, I knelt in front of him.

"Talk to me." I took his hands in mine.

"Your grandfather—"

"He knows." I told him. "As a matter of fact, he knew I had feelings for you before I admitted them. You don't have to be scared here. No one will hurt you."

"P." Wind whispered before falling against my chest to hug me. "I was so scared."

"You're safe here." I promised him.

Rubbing his back, I stood, lifting him so he could wrap his legs around my hips. Carrying him to the bed, I set him on his back and climbed over him.

I nibbled against one side of his neck, then the other making him giggle while trying to push me away.

"That tickles!" He told me. "And besides, your grandfather is downstairs."

"Downstairs." I intoned. "We're upstairs with the door closed."

I continued kissing at him—his neck, cheeks, nose.

Wind rolled us over and sat astride me looking down into my face. I folded my arms under my head while meeting his gaze. No words passed between us, but he did caress down my neck to my chest.

"I like the way your body feels." Wind admitted. "Is it because of Muay Thai?"

I nodded.

He continued down my frame, along my sides then up to reveal my tattoo.

"I even like this."

"Why do you blush when you admit that?" I asked him.

"I'm not supposed to like a man with tattoos." Wind admitted, sliding off me to sit beside me with his legs hanging off the side of the bed. "They say I'm supposed to be a good boy."

Sighing, I sat up and took his chin in my thumb and forefinger.

"How about you being a bad boy be our little secret, mm?" I teased. "So you can be as bad as you want to be."

"Behave."

"I can't help it." I nuzzled his neck. "I want you to misbehave."

His cheeks pinkened. "Let's go back before your grandfather think we're—well—you know."

I reached for him, but he was faster than I was and was running out the door before I could get to him. Laughing, I stood, stuck my hands into my pocket and followed.

We spent the next little while cooking. While dinner simmered, we took time to shower. Papa set the table and soon we were seated to eat.

"What are you studying, Wind?" Papa asked.

"Business, P." Wind replied.

"Interesting." Papa leaned forward. "Does this mean you want to start a business, or run one for someone else?"

"Well, I think I'll start by running one for someone else to get the experience." Wind told him thoughtfully. "Then once I think I'm ready, start my own hotel."

"That's great." Papa told him. "I've always respected men who want to stand on their own feet. There's something noble about that. Keep working hard."

"Thanks, P." Wind smiled brightly.

We delved into other conversations and in no time, everyone was laughing and having a good time.

My phone rang, and though I didn't want to check, I did. It could have been Kai or Bank telling me they found someone, or that the guy we'd left buried to his neck was free.

"What's wrong?" Gear asked.

"It's Pa." I replied.

Immediately, the air was sucked from the room. To avoid dampening the mood even more, I excused myself.

"Maybe I should go with him." I overheard Wind say before I stepped through the door.

175

"Not right now." Gear replied. "This is one of those things he has to face himself. You can stand by his side later."

Gear was right and I knew that as I exited the back door and stood in the darkening evening on the pool deck.

"Pa." I greeted him.

"I'll be coming into town tomorrow," he said. "I would like to speak with you and your brother."

"If you have an issue, I need you to leave Gear out of this." I told him.

"You don't have to be a gatekeeper for him anymore." My father told him. "He's an adult."

"Is that really how you think this brother thing works? I don't stop protecting him because he's an adult. Watching his back is a lifetime commitment."

"Nong."

"No. The last time I let you speak with Gear alone, you broke his heart." I snapped. "I'm not letting that happen again. If you have anything to say to Gear, you can say it in front of me."

Pa sighed. "As you wish."

I quirked a brow. "You know where to find us."

Holding my breath, I hung up and pressed my forehead to the wall.

"P?" Gear called.

I turned to see that he and Wind were standing behind me.

"What's wrong?" Wind asked.

"Pa wants to speak with us." I announced. "He'll be here tomorrow."

"I don't want to talk to him." Gear folded his arms across his chest.

"Don't worry. You won't be alone with him." I promised. "You won't have to face him alone."

Wind

The night sky was filled with stars as I laid with Storm cuddled into my side. Storm couldn't seem to get settled in the house. After a while, it was as if he couldn't catch his breath. I knew the beginning of a panic attack.

Enclosed spaces did not help with alleviating the feeling of an elephant sitting on the chest.

Papa didn't know what to do and I could see the nerves building in Gear's eyes. It was the sight of someone who wanted to help the man he loved more than anything but couldn't.

I stepped in, and suggested we slept outside.

His grandfather wasn't a fan of the plan, but we wound up convincing him.

Gear helped with the set up—beach lights stuck in the sand and turned on, a cooler with water and juice and blankets and pillows so we could be comfortable. He hugged Storm and the desperation in the hug made me walk away to give them a moment together.

Storm found me sticking my toes into the water as the waves came to die on the sand.

I felt him there but didn't turn until he hugged me from behind. He pressed his face into my neck for a quick moment before resting his chin on my shoulder.

"Are you sure you want to do this?" Storm wanted to know. "Sleeping on the floor isn't comfortable."

"I'm sure."

"You're doing this for me, Wind." Storm whispered. "The other people I dated wouldn't even—"

"I'm not the others you've dated." I told him bravely. "I'm me. And you're important to me—your wellbeing is important. It's not the worst thing to sleep on the beach."

We wandered along the water's edge, hand in hand until it was too dark before we returned to our camping spot, opened a couple bottles of juice and a bag of chips. We watched a movie on my phone then settled in for the night.

I fell asleep but was soon awake again because Storm's weight wasn't resting on my chest like he should be. I sat up and glanced around.

"P?" I called.

No answers came.

Standing, I walked toward the private beach and found him sitting, staring out over the water. I walked over to sit beside him, and he rested his head on my shoulder.

"I'm supposed to be stronger." Storm told me. "Your man is supposed to be stronger than this."

"My man is supposed to let me know when he needs help. There's no shame in admitting that."

"You're too good to be true," Storm said.

"Is there anything I can do?" I asked.

"I'll be okay." He told me. "I'm not a fan of my father's trips home."

"What does your father do?"

He shifted to look into my eyes. "You don't know?"

I shook my head.

"Really?"

"No. I don't know what your father does." I blinked. "Should I?"

"Bannasaree?"

I frowned.

"The judge?"

"P'Storm, after my father died, I barely had time to sleep much less follow the news." I shoved his shoulder. "Why would I care who your father is?"

Storm bit into his bottom lip. "Right. The last time he came, my brother thought he was here to spend time with us. He told Gear that he was grown up now and didn't need a father anymore."

"I get it now." I nodded. "When you said you never had family dinners."

"Aside from Papa and I, Gear has no family." He explained. "Our mother moved to Switzerland and created an entire new family."

"Wait—she has other kids?"

"A step-son." Storm explained. "Her and our father divorced."

"That doesn't mean she divorced you and Gear. She's your mother."

"That's precisely what it means." Storm replied. "She's been gone since the year before your father's death. She never looked back. My father only grew worse after that. The sad truth is, I think he really loved her. And to have her leave him—well, it destroyed him. He's just too proud to admit it."

"I'm sorry."

"I seem to be turning into him." Storm told me.

I didn't think he'd ever admitted that out loud before. "How so?"

"I'm cold, all the time." He cleared his throat. "Except when you hold me. Admitting my deepest feelings to you is a struggle. I want to hide it all but each time I try I feel a bit more ice grow inside me. I don't want to be him, Wind."

"You won't be."

"You're not sure."

"I'm sure." I pressed. "You're nothing like your father."

He lifted his head and turned haunted eyes at me.

"Come back to bed." I stood and extended a hand to him. "Even if you don't sleep, you can rest with me."

We settled on the blanket again and this time, I pulled him down on top of me. Bravely, I wrapped my arms around his neck and kissed him until he sighed and hugged me. When he slipped to lay beside me, I smiled at him just before he cuddled into my chest.

I remained awake.

His nightmares were a problem.

Each time he began moaning in his sleep, I held him tighter. I kissed his forehead—used my body to sooth him. At some point, I fell asleep, but it wouldn't last long. I was awakened by the waves crashing into the shore and the heat of the sun against my skin.

I didn't wake Storm.

He'd had a rough night. The longer he slept, I hoped that meant he was getting more rest to face his father.

Instead, I pulled one of the sheets over our legs since the morning was a little chilly and allowed him to sleep until he moaned and shifted against me.

"Hi." I whispered.

Storm looked up at me, smiled and held me tighter. "I'm not ready to face today yet."

"Okay, we'll stay right here until you're ready." I promised him.

"What if I'm never ready?"

"Then we'll deal with that scenario." I told him.

As promised, I stayed with him until he shifted and sat up. I knelt behind him, wrapped my arm around him from behind and kissed his neck. We stayed like that until Storm's phone went off. That was our cue to make our way back to the house.

Gear and I made breakfast for everyone while Storm showered. The younger brother was quiet which wasn't at all like him. Usually, he had his camera and was snapping pictures of everything.

"Are you okay?" I asked him.

"I'm not sure." Gear replied. "Storm spends so much of his life protecting me. It's even worse that he has to be doing it against our father. But I should be asking you if you were good with this."

"Me? I'm fine."

"Yeah—but Storm is your boyfriend."

I exhaled.

Gear was right.

I was terrified of meeting their father. I wasn't even sure if the man knew Storm was gay.

"Whatever happens, I'll stay with Storm." I promised him. "I'm not going to run off and leave him to face this man alone. He's doing everything for everyone else. It's about time someone showed him that he's not alone."

Gear hugged me.

"Um…" I wasn't sure what was happening. "What's this for?"

"Just because." Gear stepped back to pick up a large bowl of porridge. "You have my brother's back. That's all I can ever ask for."

Papa entered the room and greeted us.

"Take a seat, P." I told him while placing a plate of rice with an omelette over it in front of him.

"You can call me Papa." He beamed.

I laughed. "Sure, Papa."

"This smells amazing." Papa leaned forward to sniff at his meal. "I didn't know you cooked."

"It was nothing." I told him. "And besides, Gear helped."

"Thanks for reminding him." Gear teased. "I really shouldn't have let you cook because now you're his new favourite."

"Hey now." Papa laughed. "I love you all equally."

I grinned and was turning to head back for the rest of the rice omelets when I noticed Storm was leaning against the doorframe, watching us.

"Hungry?" I asked him.

"Hmm." He walked in to kiss my cheek and sit at the table.

Gear left the table for his camera then returned.

"Wind, I found this in the hall." Gear told me, handing me a yellow envelop. "It has your name on it."

I accepted the envelop, inspected it and arched a brow. I didn't recognize it, but it did have my name on it.

With a shrug, I shoved it into my back pocket and focused on helping him set all the food on the table, leaving some for their father.

We weren't sure when he's showed up. Apparently, he never bothered telling Storm that big of information. We delved into talks about Gear and Storm's childhoods, of days when little Storm would run around the room with Batman toys above his head, making zoom sounds.

"Batman was his favourite superhero." Gear announced.

"Please, Batman isn't a superhero." I protested. "He's a sociopath with money"

Papa laughed out loud.

Storm's eyes widened.

"What?" I asked.

"How dare you, sir!" Storm teased, flicking my shoulder with a finger. "He is too a superhero."

"Okay, what superpowers does he have?" I asked, pouting at him.

"Money." Storm rationalized.

We laughed out loud again.

"Somehow, I don't think that's how it works." Gear pointed out.

As we had fun, Gear took pictures of all of us—and eventually set the camera on the counter behind us.

"All I'm saying is Batman is pretty cool." Storm chewed.

I scrunched my nose and shook my head.

"Okay, who is your favourite superhero?" Papa asked.

"I never had one." I shrugged. "The only ones I knew were Superman, Batman and the Black Panther. I was partial to the Black Panther. His moves were awesome."

Everyone at the table groaned and I smirked.

"Disapproval." Gear cheered.

"You guys are jerks." I accused.

"Every little boy needs a superhero—a fictional one—I have tons of the comics if you want to read them." Papa offered.

The conversation switched to other fun things until the family album came out. I giggled at pictures of Storm with his head shaved because he made a girl angry at school and she stuck gum in his hair. Storm blushed and shook his head.

"You're not cute bald." I laughed.

"This is not okay." Storm leaned over to press his face to my shoulder.

"I'm getting to know you better from the people who know you best." I defended Papa and Gear.

Gear told another funny story, and we were all laughing when a voice sounded from the door.

Storm and Gear turned toward it and the happiness drained from their face. I shifted closer to Storm and wanted to reach for Gear, but the younger brother merely rose, offered the man wai and carried his plates to the sink.

"I'll help you wash up," Gear told me as he picked up my plate as well.

Storm didn't move.

Papa exhaled.

"Come in." Papa motioned to the only other chair. "The boys made breakfast."

When I turned to gather a plate for the newcomer, Storm rose and took it from my hand. I secretly touched his cheek for a second and he smiled sadly at me.

Gear picked up his camera and headed for the door.

"Go with him for me." Storm told me.

"I don't want to leave you."

"Please—he needs someone." Storm pleaded. "For me."

I stared at him silently, a million thoughts going through my mind.

Reluctantly, I nodded and followed Gear out of the room. He didn't stop and I followed him out of the house and down to the beach where he tilted his head back and shouted as if trying to unburden.

He did it twice more before exhaling loudly and looking at me.

"We can go back now." Gear told me.

Nodding, I walked by his side back toward the house.

"It must have taken years for the relationship between Storm and your father to get this bad." I pointed out.

"It was never the best." Gear replied. "But it got worse when my father started treating me the way he treated Storm. My big brother can be very protective."

"I know."

"No, you don't." Gear sighed and stopped walking. "When he finds whoever attacked you—"

"Will he kill them?"

"He'll want to." Gear replied.

"Gear!"

"Don't worry." Gear shook his head. "He won't. But they're going to wish he did."

"Maybe he won't find them."

Gear chuckled. "My brother has the Bannarasee name and more money than Midas. Trust me, he'll find them."

I was immediately sick to my stomach.

"I think my brother's love for you will be the only thing that will save them." Gear started walking again. "You don't understand how angry he was when he walked into that hospital."

"You think he loves me?" I wanted to know.

"Everyone sees it." Gear laughed.

"He hasn't said anything."

"Storm is a little cautious. You're his first guy, you know."

I cleared my throat and caught his arm. "He's dated before, right? Girls."

"Yeah." Gear leaned his back against the rail and faced me. "But none of them ever worked. He's never brought any of them home to meet Papa. I met one of them and there was nothing there."

"Meaning?"

"Meaning, she was falling all over him, and Storm just looked as if he wanted to be anywhere but there." Gear explained. "The test of Storm's seriousness for you isn't meeting Pa."

"It's meeting Papa."

Gear nodded. "Papa was the one who taught us all we needed to learn about relationships and love. We've built what we deserve after his love for our grandmother. Storm learned what it was to be family from Papa. He learned how to be a man from Papa, and I learned from both of them."

We sat on the final step for a moment.

"He's my first guy too." I told Gear. "I mean, I knew I was gay, but I haven't been brave enough to actually go out with someone. And besides, I live in a small village."

"Dating pool a bit small?"

I laughed. "Something like that. The truth is, if Storm hadn't been so determined, I don't think I'd ever get over my shyness."

"I don't think so." Gear shrugged. "We are all shy, but people date."

"Trust me, there's something about Storm that made me give in."

"I couldn't ask for a better big brother." Gear told me soberly. "Sometimes he can be a pain in the butt—but he means well. Realizing what he caused you almost killed him. He wouldn't get out of bed for days."

I hung my head.

"Have you forgiven him for that?"

"Mmm."

"You have?" Gear asked.

"I'm here, aren't I?"

"There you two are." Papa's voice caused us to stand and turned toward him. "Come inside. Gear, join your father and brother in the office."

"Papa." Gear pleaded.

"Storm won't leave you." Papa promised.

Gear exhaled loudly, handed me his camera and disappeared into the house.

"I don't like this, Papa." I admitted to the older man.

"I know, Nong." He nodded and patted my shoulder as I walked by him into the house. "I know."

Storm

The way I wanted to ask Wind to be my boyfriend wasn't the way I'd asked him to be. In my head, the moment would be romantic—maybe over a nice dinner, or a date to the beach, or even on stage during one of our shows. I wanted it to be something he remembered as one of the best moments of his life.

As I sat in front of my father, waiting for Gear to enter so we could get this game he seemed to be playing over with, I thought back to holding Wind, of the fear I felt when I received that phone call from Bank.

I wondered for a moment if that was how my father felt when my mother told him she was leaving. I was always looking for reasons as to why my father became the kind of father he had.

He wasn't the most attentive to begin with, but he at least showed up for things—birthdays, graduations, award ceremonies. After mother left, everything in him, every fatherly instinct inside him went away with my mother.

Those thoughts have become strong since Wind—wanting to understand the mistakes my parents made so I didn't make them with Wind.

"Pa, you asked to see us." I leaned forward.

"Gear wants nothing to do with me." Pa said.

"He shows you respect." I pointed out. "If nothing else, Papa and I taught him that."

Pa bowed his head and breathed loudly before speaking. "I suppose. But that's not entirely what I—"

"In all fairness, you cannot walk into this house and demand anything else. Gear spent most of the time curled up in my arms at nights, crying, wondering why he wasn't good enough. As his big brother, I have to make sure he is okay, that he has all the tools he needs so he will be fine if I'm not around. That wasn't my job. My job was to love him, to tease him. You were supposed to make him into a man."

"My heart was broken." My father admitted. "All I could do was work—I didn't think I had anything else."

"You had me." I pointed out. "You had me and Gear. Our hearts were broken too. Our mother was gone—the woman who was supposed to love us more than anything else. Pa, we were hurting too."

"*P. kho tod, na?*" His voice trembled. "I didn't think about that."

Gear entered the room then and I leaned back. Instead of taking the seat next to our father, he opted for sitting on the floor in front of my legs. Before he turned to sit, however, I saw the fear and confusion in his eyes.

I touched his head, and he lifted a hand to pat mine gently before bringing his legs up to wrap his arms around his knees.

"You have our attention, Pa," I said.

He inhaled a shaky breath and laced his fingers. "I don't know if you remember Rong Manaraporn." Pa began watching Gear closely. "He passed away last week."

Gear and I exchanged glances.

"When he died, he left some things a mess." Pa continued. "Especially things with his daughters. It made me realize that I've wasted the relationship I could have had with the two of you."

Neither Gear nor I said anything. I was beginning to think this whole thing was a joke. Gear shifted so he could rest his back against my legs, but other than that he made no movement.

"Seeing what his family is going through—what his kids are going through—it scares me." Pa went on. "So much so that I took a couple of days out of the city to think about how we are with each other, and I want to fix things with us."

Gear laughed. "This is a nightmare. I'm going to fall off the bed any second now and the pain will push me back into reality."

"I know the both of you have no reason to trust me," Pa said. "But I can't live forever and I don't want to leave this earth with the two of you angry."

"Pa, this shouldn't be about your peace of mind." Gear pointed out. "P'Storm and I did nothing wrong. Yet we've suffered—we are suffering because the adults in this equation stopped loving each other. P has given up his teenage years to raise me. He should have been out dating, partying learning—but he was here at nights, homework checks, helping me with broken hearts, pushing me to grow, to be better—he sacrificed his life for me."

Pa said nothing.

"Buying us a condo and forcing your older son to raise your younger one while you live in an entirely different city is not parenting." Gear seemed as though he had all of this pent up inside him.

It was almost as if he'd been waiting for a long time to unload the burden of my father's irresponsibility.

Usually, I'd stop him, but it didn't seem to be healthy for him, letting all that fester. This time, I'd let him unburden.

"And P'Storm won't say anything but it hurts him. Do you think I like seeing my brother in pain, Pa?" Gear sniffled and used the back of his hand to rub his nose.

I rested a hand on his shoulder and Gear rubbed his cheek against it then leveled his stare on our father who was watching us.

"Tell me how to fix this." Pa told us.

"Words mean nothing, Pa." I finally spoke up. "I'm old enough now to not be worried about a father but Gear still cares about you. I won't let you hurt him again."

"Is he right?" Pa asked. "Did you give up your teenage years?"

"No." I told him. "I didn't give up my teenage years."

"P…" Gear pleaded.

"Giving up the years meant I had a choice." I corrected my father. "I don't regret taking care of my brother. He is the love of my life. But you had no right to put that on my shoulders. No matter how many lifetimes I have—no matter how many times I get put in that situation, I'll make the same decision. But you have to stand up now."

"Does that mean you're leaving me, P?" Gear turned to kneel in front of me. "That you're leaving me to him?"

I framed his face. "Never."

"You promise?"

I smiled. "Promise."

"P." Gear leaned forward to rest his forehead to my chest. "I don't want to."

I rested a gentle palm to the back of his head. I could almost feel the exhausted pain vibrating against his head. "You heard him."

Gear rose and left the room. I waited until he closed the door before I said anything else.

"Getting him back won't happen over-night." I explained. "He's in pain, the same hurt I've tried protecting him from. You're going to have to give him time and let him come to you."

"And what about you?"

"I don't know, P." I shook my head. "I have a safe space."

"Because you have—him?"

"The only reason I'm even speaking to you right now is because of him." I licked my suddenly dried lips. "He sees something in me, and I can't let him down. He makes me strong."

"Your boyfriend."

"So, you *have* been keeping tabs on us."

"I didn't have to." Pa replied. "But I thought about it."

"Then how do you know that Wind is my boyfriend?"

Pa sighed. "I used to look at your mother the way he looks at you. The only thing is, she never, ever looked at me the way N'Wind looks at you. I guess that should have been a red flag."

I sighed. "I don't think I have to say this, Pa. But wind is off limits."

"I want the best for you, and he comes from nothing."

"Do you think I care that he has no money?" I leaned forward, ensuring he saw the absolute rage in my eyes. "He's done more for me just by standing at my side than anyone else. If I find out, that you do anything to make him even think of being sad—I will ruin you."

"I'm your father."

"You're my DNA." I informed him while rising to my feet. "There's a difference."

Tugging my shirt back in place, I left the room. In the kitchen, Wind hurried over to hold me as I looked around the room to find Gear.

"In his bedroom." Papa told me. "Are you all right?"

I kissed the top of Wind's head while nodding.

Wind was fussing over me when my father walked into the room. That didn't seem to matter to Wind as he merely framed my face, smiled up at me and pulled me back into his arms.

"You're okay, P." Wind told me repeatedly. "You're okay."

"I'm not going back to the city." Pa told the room. "I've decided to stay here."

"Not here." Papa told him. "This house is their safe zone—I can't allow you to take that away from them."

"Papa." I chided him.

"He's my son, and I love him. But no." Papa set his cane against his chair.

"It's fine." Pa sighed. "I have a place nearby already."

191

I held my breath but Wind secretly locking his pinky with mine calmed me.

"Okay, that's enough for today." Papa picked up his cane and pushed to his feet.

Before I could, Wind hurried over to help him. I took the time to turn to my father who was watching my boyfriend and grandfather intently.

Though I wanted to use the bathroom, I remained in the room. I had no intentions of leaving my father in a room, alone, with Wind.

"N'Wind, how about accompanying an old man on a walk?" Papa asked.

Wind looked over at me. "I promised—"

I smiled. "Go." I told him. "You and I can have some time together later."

"That's not—" Wind paused to look over at Papa.

"He doesn't want to leave you with me." Pa spoke up. "I get it. I'm going to leave. We can talk later."

I said nothing.

Pa left us then and though I wanted to kiss Wind for standing up for me and by me, I couldn't—not in front of Papa.

I watched Wind walk with Papa out the door then ran up the stairs to check on Gear. He was curled up in bed, cuddling a large bear I'd given to him when he was twelve. I pulled the sheets up to his shoulders, kissed his forehead and closed the door behind me as I left the room.

In my room, I sat on the bed and called Kai.

"Wait, your father thought he could have a say in who you're with now?" Kai asked.

I sighed. "I can't crumble under this, Kai. But I feel like I'm about to."

"Listen, do you need me?" Kai asked.

"I'm good right now."

"And Gear..." Kai's voice cracked.

The softness in his voice made me smile. It seemed my best friend had a crush. Though I could be wrong.

"He's sleeping." I replied. "I think dealing with my father took it out of him. But he's fine. Don't worry—I have his back."

Kai sighed. "You're coming back tomorrow as planned?"

"Yeah. We have to. I don't think Wind can miss anymore classes."

"Call if you need anything." Kai advised me. "If anything changes."

I promised I would, and I wasn't sure when it happened, but I fell asleep. It wasn't until Wind crawled into my arms a while later, that I woke up. His hair tickled my nose as he tossed a possessive arm across my midsection and rested his head on my chest.

Welcoming his closeness, I drifted off to sleep again.

The next time I opened my eyes, Wind was sitting on the floor packing our bags. Sitting up in the bed, I shimmied to the edge and kissed his neck. Wind laughed, reached back to ruffle my hair, then when back to what he was doing.

"I figured I should do this now, save us some time tomorrow." Wind explained.

"I would have preferred you be in bed with me when I woke up." I nuzzled his neck from behind again. "But this is productive."

"Are you and Gear really okay?" Wind turned to look at me.

I nodded. "We're okay. I mean, it's going to be a fight, but I think we can do it."

"P, I worry about you."

Climbing off the bed, I turned him to face me. I drew in as close as we could and rested my forehead to his. "Pa wants to make amends. Right now, Gear isn't ready and I'm not forcing him to. All I can do is be there for him."

"And while you're there for him." Wind rested a comforting hand on my chest. "I'll be there for you."

We gathered that night for a family dinner—and though our father's visit still hung in the air, Gear seemed better. He sat beside Papa while I sat beside Wind and we enjoyed our final few hours before bed. Gear and I sat on the deck to have a drink while Wind browsed Papa's books.

He sat on the deck and rested his head on my lap, staring up at the sky.

"Do you think we'll ever be able to get married?" Gear asked.

"I don't know." I replied. "Maybe not in the *normal* sense of the word, like legally. But we can have a ceremony in front of those who love us."

"And will that be enough?"

I thought about it for a while then looked down to brush some hair from Gear's forehead. "It will have to be for us. As long as we push things a little further—make it easier on our children."

"Children?" Gear sat up to watch me. "You want children?"

"Mmm. Don't you?"

"We're gay, P."

"There are ways." I promised him. "But you're entirely too young to be thinking about that now. Come on, you should get some sleep. The ride back will be a long one."

Gear kissed the side of my head and left me alone. For the first time in the last few days, I exhaled and lifted my gaze upward.

I wasn't sure what was going to happen next. All I knew, was Wind and Gear had to be safe, protected. Before our father waltzed back into our lives, I thought I had a handle on things.

But the moment I saw his name on my phone, I knew that was only a false sense of security.

I called Wind's mother.

"Nong?" She asked, shock in her voice. "Is Wind okay?"

194

"He's fine." I replied. "I know we aren't supposed to say this—but I'm feeling a little overwhelmed and I could use a mother."

"Oh, sweetie. Tell me what's going on."

I explained it to her, and she made a sympathetic sound in her throat.

"The answer really is quite simple." Mae told me.

"It is?"

"Of course." Mae replied. "As parents we forget that we can't raise our children the way we were raised. We forget the times are different and the pressures have multiplied since we were your age. It's because of this lapse in judgement that our children suffer."

I sighed.

"You know this information now." Mae continued. "And you now have my son who will be there for you. Accept that embrace. You lean on those around you and if you have to come home—come home."

"Home?"

"To me." Mae told me.

Tears tumbled down my cheeks. I buried my face in my hand.

"Do you hear me?" Mae asked.

I couldn't form any words.

"N'Storm?" She demanded.

"I hear you." My voice cracked.

"You heard me what?"

"Mae."

"Good." Mae exhaled. "Now, you're going to stand up and you're going to be better than your parents, better than me."

"Mae." I managed. "Thank you."

"Oh, sweetheart. There's nothing to thank me for."

When I hung up the phone, I wandered into the house to find Wind sitting in my bed, reading.

The moment he saw me, he closed the book and opened his arms to me. Without hesitating, I climbed into bed, half my body on top of his and cuddled my head under his chin. He rubbed my back, and I closed my eyes.

"Are you okay?" Wind asked.

"I am now." I replied. "I'm right where I should be."

We passed the night watching a movie then tried sleeping.

Wind fell asleep holding my hand.

A few times, I lifted the hand to my lips for a kiss, wondering when the next shoe would fall and tear us apart.

I knew he was still worried about what people thought of him with me. That problem didn't go away because life threw other wrenches into the works of it all. I wouldn't be letting go—we'd just have to find some other way of dealing with it.

The truth was, I didn't care what people thought about us. I knew how hard I had to fight to get Wind to give me a second look. He didn't care I had money—now when he looks at me, I see the realness of his feelings, although he didn't say them out loud.

I felt them warm me like the rays of a thousand suns every time he held me, smiled at me—every time he reached out and took my hand.

He was my happy place, and I prayed every moment of every day that I was the same comfort for him.

I drifted in and out of sleep until morning and when I did open my eyes, it was to the smell of coffee and the softness of Wind's lips moving across my jawline and hairline. I moaned and wrapped my arms around him, pulling him down to the bed and under my body.

Wind giggled as I sniff-kissed his neck and cheeks.

"You two!" Gear called out, laughter rich in his voice.

"Sorry, Gear." Wind called, trying to push at my chest.

"I regret nothing." I nipped at his neck, causing him to laugh out loud.

"That tickles." Wind squealed.

"Ugh!" Gear protested. "I'll leave you two alone. Just remember we're heading back today so, whatever it is you two are going to do to each other, make it quick."

"Wait!" Wind called, pushing him off. "We're not going to be doing anything!"

"Speak for yourself." I caught him around the waist as he moved to get off the bed and pulled him back in my arms. "I want to do all the things."

"P'Storm! Don't be naughty."

I groaned my disappointment but released him. He was leaving the room before stopping and turning back to sit on the side of the bed.

"P."

"Hmm?"

"About intimacy."

I pushed up to my elbow. "I told you, I can wait."

"Yes, but for how long?"

"For as long as it takes." I assured him.

"It's not that I'm a prude." Wind bowed his head. "I just—I'm scared."

"Of me?"

"No." He dragged his palm down my arm. 'How can I be scared of you? It's just—weren't you scared your first time?"

"This is still my first time, Wind." I admitted. "I've never been with a guy before. So, when the time comes, we can be scared together."

"Wait—you're scared?"

I nodded.

"It should be like riding a bike, right?" Wind teased.

I laughed. "This is nothing like riding a bike. But we'll figure it out."

Wind kissed my arm. "Let's go before Gear and Papa eat all the breakfast."

Though he exited the room, I flopped back to the pillows for a moment, thinking of making love with Wind. Though it terrified me, I knew I was ready—I wanted to.

I closed my eyes and allowed my brain to drift back to his kisses.

Yes, I definitely wanted to.

Wind

Bank jumped on my back the moment he saw me. Laughing, I gave him a ride to the tables before he hopped off. Though people stared, I didn't care. I hugged him then sat beside him at one of the tables.

"So—how was it?" Banks asked.

"I told him everything. By the time I was finished, his eyes were wide.

"Yup." I told him.

"Well, the upside is you got meeting the father out of the way."

"Right." I scoffed. "But can I talk to you about something?"

Bank arched a brow and leaned closer. "Of course."

"Um, is it too soon to say I'm in love with P'Storm?"

Bank shook his head. "No. From what I know—my father fell in love with my mother the second he saw her. I mean love doesn't have a timeline."

I nodded.

"Have you told him?"

I shook my head. "I can't. He's going through enough as is. Plus, he just asked me to be his boyfriend. I'm going to wait and see."

"Well, my birthday is coming up." Bank told me. "Want to come by the hotel for the weekend? *Base Note* will be performing—every couple could do with a little alone time."

"Alone time?" I sputtered. "As in…"

Bank smirked. "Being with someone shouldn't be something you're ashamed of. And being *with* him should be a good thing."

"When you say *with* him…" I looked around then back at my friend. "Have you ever been with anyone?"

"Yes, remember? It wasn't—I wasn't in love with him."

"Him?"

Bank nodded. "My point is, being with that one person wasn't right. It didn't feel right but I did it because I didn't want to lose him. I lost him anyway. My father said it wasn't meant to be. And I took some comfort in that."

"You're saying don't sleep with P'Storm if I don't feel it's right."

Bank nodded.

"N'Wind?"

Gift's voice was now like a bad taste in my mouth.

"Could we go somewhere and talk?" Gift wanted to know.

"Not today, Satan." Bank rose from his seat to glare at Gift.

"Are you his bodyguard or something?" Gift asked.

"When P'Storm isn't around? Yes." Bank told her.

"Wind?" Gift looked at me.

Instead of speaking with her, I picked up my bag, climbed from behind the table and headed off toward the business department.

Bank jogged to catch up with me and wrapped an arm around my shoulder, checking if I was okay.

"Let me ruin her life." Bank pleaded. "Please! Just give me the word."

"No." I replied. "I have a bad feeling about her now. Every time she's around I get this feeling in the pit of my stomach."

Bank glanced back but I couldn't get myself to.

The rest of the day went by in a blur. We finished filming the last couple of scenes from the movie. Seua rewrote the script to kill off Gift's character to save himself from having to recast her and refilm the scenes she was already in.

It was a genius idea.

With the film wrapped, we all went out for dinner, but Storm and I didn't stay the whole night. Knowing Kai would bring Gear home, Storm and I climbed into his car and headed for the dorm.

"Bank says his birthday was coming." I stuck my hand out the window, loving the wind floating through my fingers and over my skin. "*Base Note* will be playing it. He says that you and I could have a weekend together at the hotel."

"Really?"

"Yes, really." I replied. "Being away from the city could be good for us."

"But I'll be working." Storm reminded me. "Set up, rehearsals, actually performing—when will we have time?"

I sighed dramatically.

"Do you want alone time with me?" Storm asked as he pulled into the parking lot at the dorms.

I didn't reply until after he'd turned off the ignition and removed his seatbelt.

"Of course." I replied.

"Then I'll make it happen."

Even after we got back to the room, I wasn't sure how he'd make that happen. With the amount of work we both had to do until the end of the semester, I didn't want to overload him with my need to being close to him.

Storm kissed my neck and closed himself into the bathroom. I busied myself with pushing our beds together. I hadn't asked Storm if he wanted to—I was simply taking a chance.

When he exited, I was standing by the window, staring out into the darkness. He walked up behind me and wrapped his arms around to press his palms to my chest.

"Go shower." He told me.

"Will you wait for me?"

"Mmm."

It was hard to peel myself from his arms, but I did and headed into the shower. I made it a quick one, dressed in a pair of shorts and a t-shirt then exited the bathroom to find Storm sitting on our bed, laptop in front of him.

I dragged the towel back and forth on my head, trying to get my hair to stop dripping. "What are you doing?"

"Checking emails." He responded without looking at me. "They pile up when you don't check them for three days."

"Anything good?"

"Not really." He replied. "Mostly school stuff."

Storm closed the laptop and put it away then took my hand. When he took the towel and began rubbing my head, I rested backward against his chest.

The days rolled by.

My mother and I texted back and forth while Storm and the rest of his guys prepared for Bank's birthday celebration.

We arrived at the hotel to hugs from Pretty, her boyfriend and Bank's father.

While they skirted Storm and the rest of the band off, I was left to be company for the others. I missed Storm, but I knew this was something he had to do. With that thought firmly in mind, I exhaled and settled into enjoying myself and the new friends I'd made.

Base Note performed and everyone was happy. The only down side was I didn't have a moment alone with Storm except at night. By then he'd been so exhausted, he merely fell asleep while I showered.

I didn't have the heart to wake him. After kissing his forehead, I snuggled into his side and closed my eyes.

Saturday didn't give us time either—*Base Note* was talked into an impromptu concert. Storm asked me if he could take it—I didn't hesitate. I kissed him and told him to go with his friends.

Sunday night, I gave up and we drove back to the dorms and this time, I fell asleep while Storm showered.

The next morning, I woke up, he was gone.

I sighed, tossed one of the pillows across the room.

Lazily, I got up, showered, and dressed.

I wandered to the campus, fell into a seat beside Bank and pulled my books out.

Bank handed me a snack bar but didn't say anything. I couldn't focus so I secretly recorded the lecture.

When we walked out of the class, Seua was there to get me. Apparently, Storm wanted to meet with me and Bank. We then made our way into a fancy neighbourhood.

I wasn't sure where we were, but Storm was standing at the entrance as we entered the large gates and parked.

Hopping from the car, I jogged up to kiss him. He took my hands in his and smiled sadly at me.

"What's this place?" I asked.

"It's Gear's." He replied.

"Gear owns a house?" I asked. "Then why does he live in a condo close to the school?"

"It's closer." Storm replied. "Listen, there's something we have to do in order for us to move on."

Seua, and Bank walked by us and disappeared inside.

"Okay?"

Storm cleared his throat, lifted my hands to kiss the backs then met my gaze again. "Do you remember me promising I'd find out who attacked you?"

I nodded.

"I found out who attacked you, but they did it because they were hired to." Storm explained. "We found out who hired them."

"Who?"

"Come with me."

Silently, I allowed him to take my hand and led me further into the house after closing the front door.

We passed through a couple of beautiful spaces, but I didn't have time to check it all out. When I entered a larger room, I stopped, and my hand slipped from his.

"You?" I asked.

"It's okay." Storm replied.

"P'Storm?" I asked looking up at him.

"Gift hired thugs to attack you." Storm explained. "Want to know why?"

"Let her tell me." I slowly eased into the room. "Let her explain to me. You said you loved me—is this what you do to someone you love?"

"Why should he have you?" Gift asked.

"Why should that be your issue who has me?" I countered. "You knew from the very beginning that I wasn't into you. You don't love me."

"But I do!" She grabbed my hand.

I yanked my arm back and pushed her away from me. "Don't ever say that! I almost died."

"You weren't going to die." Gift assured me. "I told them not to kill you."

"Oh! You did!" I scoffed. "That makes it so much better!"

Exhaling, I glanced around the room at my new friends. They were all standing, as if waiting for her to do something stupid. I looked up into Storm's eyes, touched his cheek gently making him smile down at me.

"Don't touch him like that." Gift looked away. "Not while I'm here."

"I don't care what you feel." I turned around to look at her. "And usually, I would talk P'Storm down. But I'm going to step out of the way. I'm new to this boyfriend thing, but I'm pretty sure he's supposed to protect me as I protect him."

"Wind?" Storm asked.

"You're up."

Storm smiled—the kind of smile an evil genius did before he blew up the world.

"Have a seat, Gift." Storm told her.

"What're you going to do to me?" Gift asked as she fell into a chair.

"Do you know what the penalty is for hiring someone to hurt someone else?" Storm asked. "Because I do."

"And how would you know?"

Storm leaned forward then hunched down and pulled out his phone. He dialed and I walked over to sit by Kai's feet.

Kai gripped my shoulder affectionately, and I touched his hand, smiled up at him then turned to see what was happening.

Bank fell into the sofa beside us, and we all just watch quietly.

Though there was a small voice in the back of my head telling me to show her mercy. A louder voice reminded me she could have had me killed.

I could have died.

"You can come in now," Storm said then hung up. "You see, Gift, what I wanted to do was burn your world to the ground. I wanted to turn the screws and watch you squirm. But you see, my boyfriend has a heart. And he always wants me to do the right thing."

The front door opened, and we heard footsteps coming toward us.

"You say you love him." Storm continued. "When I was a little boy, my Papa always read this thing to me."

Storm shuffled a little closer to her. Before continuing to speak.

"Love is patient. Love is kind." Storm exhaled. "It does not envy. It does not boast. It is not proud. It does not dishonor others. It is not self-seeking. It is not easily angered. It keeps no records of wrong. Love does not delight in evil but rejoices with truth. It always protects, always trusts, always hopes, always persevere."

"Wh-what does that mean?" Gift asked as the footsteps grew louder.

I looked toward the door to see Storm's father along with two police officers.

"Always protects, Gift." Storm repeated. "Love always protects—and I'm going to protect Wind from everything and everyone who wants to harm him."

"Judge Bannasaree." Gift's voice cracked as she tried backing away, causing her chair to tumble over backward. "No."

"My name is Klahan Bannasaree." Storm told her.

"No." Gift muttered. "No, it can't—it can't be."

"Allow me to introduce you to my father." Storm spoke, rising to his full height and walking around the overturned chair to look down at Gift. "You remember what he said about anyone who comes after his child."

"I didn't." She shrieked. "I didn't go after his child!"

"No?" Storm asked. "Wind is my heart. You went after him."

"What's going to happen to me?" She sobbed.

"I don't know." Pa spoke up. "We'll let the courts decide. But after your accomplice testifies—well, I can hazard a guess."

"Please!" She pleaded. "Don't let them take me. Wind, please!"

"Your actions have consequences, P." I told her. "These are them."

"I'm begging you!"

I simply rose from the floor to sit on the sofa.

No one had to tell me that I should feel something for Gift in this moment. For better or worse she had been my first friend in university. But I couldn't forgive her for what she'd done.

Storm walked over to hold my hand as the police officers arrested Gift.

As she screeched for help being dragged out of the room, I turned my face into his neck. Though it shouldn't, watching Gift being hauled away broke my heart.

Storm held onto me, his arms tight around me, the way I liked it.

"Is she really going to jail?" Seua asked.

"Yes." Storm replied. "I think she watches too many dramas where the females do these irresponsible things and get away with it."

"Putting someone's life in danger like that is not okay." Kai added. "They could have killed Wind."

"Agreed." Seua nodded.

"At least now." Storm pressed a hand to the back of my head. "I don't have to worry. Are you okay, love?"

I nodded and stood back to look up at Storm. "Thanks for not hurting her."

Storm smiled. "I wanted to. But you wouldn't have approved."

I kissed him.

"Now what do we do?" Kai asked.

"Now." Storm took my arm and twirled me around then pulled me into his chest. "We finished the week and I take my boyfriend away for the weekend."

"And I know the perfect place." Bank smirked.

"All of you are supposed to be protecting me." I pointed out. "You're supposed to not leave me alone with him."

"Well." Seua stepped up. "If anyone else tries to hurt you then we have your back. Storm on the other hand...well—well, you know."

"We're going to head back." Kai stood. "I'm going to bum a ride back with Bank. You have the cycle. There's an extra helmet strapped to the back for Wind."

Kai winked as he patted me on the shoulder.

Before I knew it, everyone else was gone, leaving me alone with Storm. He gave me the tour of the house and as dusk fell, we cooked together.

My mother video called us in the middle of making dinner and we both stopped what we were doing to talk to her.

Afterward, Storm felt left out. We called Papa, who lit up the moment he saw us.

We settled on the floor, with candles lit around us as we ate. Storm told me stories about his grandmother. He spoke about her as if she was a queen—he knew she loved him dearly and he beamed when he spoke of her.

"She sounds like an angel." I told him.

"She was." He sighed. "I just—I'm afraid I'll forget her."

"She lives through you." I told him, leaning backward into the warm, safety of his embrace.

"It doesn't feel like it sometimes."

"Makes sense." I told him. "But, every time you tell stories about her, she lives on. Tell the stories to Gear, to me. We'll make sure you don't forget."

Storm sighed. "You're wonderful."

"Why are you complimenting me?" I asked.

"It's the truth." Storm dropped his mouth to my neck then to nibble against my shoulder.

I melted for him, sighed and dropped my head to the side so he could have better access.

I loved when he nibbled at me, nipped at my skin, especially the spot just beneath my ears. When he pulled my earlobe into his mouth, I whispered his name, and a beautifully warm tremor traced my spine.

He rolled me to the floor and rose over me, beautiful with his dark eyes seeing through my soul. I tangled my arms around his neck, my fear of him, or of being intimate with him vanishing like mist in a windstorm.

"Are you still scared?" I asked him.

"No—I just want you."

As the candlelight flickered around us, he dragged a palm down my side to my thigh. He lifted it, spreading me open and falling intimately against me. Though my cheeks heated, I simply sat up to kiss him.

Storm eased away from me to catch his breath. "Hold on."

"Hold on? P'Storm?"

"I just lost control."

"I'm not complaining." I sat up to touch his cheek.

"I didn't have a choice about how I asked you out." Storm told me. "I wanted it to be romantic—special."

"You asked me." I whispered. "That's all that matters."

"I want these memories for you to be good." Storm explained.

"Do you think ten years from now I'll remember the finer details?" I wanted to know. "All I'll remember is that I was with you—that my first time was with you."

"Can you please do me this one favor?" Storm asked.

I exhaled loudly but nodded. "Okay."

"Just a little bit longer."

"*Khrap.*"

We spent the night together in the silence of the large house. We came as close to making love as we could, but I knew this was important to Storm—the wait. He wanted our first moment together to be as perfect as possible.

When we fell asleep, it was well into the morning and soon afterward we had to be up and rushing back to the dorms so we could make it to class on time. I didn't mind. When he dropped me at my campus, I kissed him as many times as I could.

Students stared.

They whispered.

When I walked into my class with Bank, I realized why they were whispering. They news had spread that Gift had been arrested, that she was facing some serious charges for what happened to me.

They knew about the video footage and that the thug confessed. The other thug was missing and a part of me knew Kai and Storm had something to do with that.

I said nothing.

I fell into the seat beside Bank who bounced me with his shoulder.

"P'Storm needs to be a lot gentler." Bank whispered.

"What?"

He pointed to my neck.

Using the camera on my phone, I held it up like a mirror to inspect my neck. When I saw what Bank was pointing at, my eyes widened.

Dark spots were at the base of my neck just above my shoulder. I tried pulling my collar up but that didn't work to hide it.

"Don't hide it." Bank winked at me. "Wear it like a badge of honour."

I groaned. "Do you think anyone else saw it?"

"I'm pretty sure they've seen it." Bank laughed. "You worry too much."

"Let me ask you something—were you in on finding Gift?" I asked him.

"Yes. And I know I should have told you." Bank exhaled. "But P'Storm didn't want you to worry. He cares about you, and I agreed with him."

I didn't have a chance to reply. Our teacher entered then, and I had to focus on what was happening with the class. Bank stuck with me until the end and just before he headed for his car, he stopped me.

"I know you said you wanted a weekend alone with P'Storm." Bank leaned in to whisper. "My dad has a suite for you next weekend."

"I don't know if P'Storm is free then."

"Trust me, he'll make time." Bank winked at me and took off jogging toward the parking lot.

"Bank!" I called.

He merely waved over his shoulder.

Shaking my head, I headed across campus.

I stopped to pick up some snacks then made my way to Storm's campus. I wasn't sure where he was, and I intended on surprising him. I made my way through the front doors and looked up at the vast staircase then down the corridors.

"Wind!"

I turned to see Gear walking toward me.

"What are you doing here?" Gear asked after a hug.

"I wanted to surprise P'Storm."

"I'll take you to him." Gear told me.

"How are you doing?" I asked him. "We haven't really had a chance to talk since your father."

"I'm okay. P'Kai took me to the beach. I had a chance to scream my head off—get some stress out."

"P'Kai, huh?"

Gear said nothing. When I looked over at him, his cheeks were red, but he still didn't say anything.

I didn't push it.

Gear was young—though older than I was by a year, he was still young. He had some time before he needed to be worried about finding someone.

I smiled as we stopped in front of a room and Gear pulled out his phone. When his phone went off again, he nodded and shoved it into his pocket.

"Come on." Gear opened the door and we entered.

Seua, Kai, Storm and a couple other students were in the room at the same table. When I entered, one of them turned to arch a brow at me.

"The infamous N'Wind." He smirked.

I blushed.

"It's okay." The other said. "We know who you're here to see."

"Down boys." Storm rose and walked over to me.

"I brought you some snacks." I told him. "I know you'll be studying late."

"Are you going to be okay going home to an empty house?" Storm asked.

I laughed softly. "I'll be fine." Leaning upward, I whispered in his ear. "We have a date next weekend."

Storm took my hand and led me from the room so we could speak in private.

"We have a date?" Storm asked.

"Yes—all weekend. Just you and me."

Storm bowed his head as his cheeks pinkened. When he looked at me again, he licked his lips and backed me into the nearest wall.

"Are you in, P'Storm?" I teased, turning my head to nip at his cheek.

"Oh—I'm so in!"

Storm

It was late when we left the city and headed toward the hotel. Wind insisted on us stopping at the mall and that I stayed with the car. I wasn't sure what he went in for, but when he came back, he quickly shoved his purchase into his backpack and shoved it between his legs on the floor.

I hadn't stayed with the car. I'd gone into the mall to pick something up and had hidden it in my bag. I wanted to surprise him.

The drive to the hotel took about an hour and the moment we arrived, we were ushered to a beautiful view of the ocean. Wind and I showered together and as many times as we'd done that, he still blushed.

While he dried his hair, I ordered room service and had it ready by the time he was finished. We ate together, sitting on the floor of our bedroom. This was such a simple thing, but it made me feel as if I belonged to someone.

As we ate dessert, I pulled out what I'd purchased at the mall and set the velvet box on his thigh.

"P?"

"Mmm?"

"What is this?" Wind asked. "Open it and find out."

I watched as he picked up the box in shaking hands and lifted the lid. Wind looked up at me, then down at the necklace in the box.

"Is this for me?" Wind asked. "It looks expensive."

I smiled. "I wanted to give you something that every time you look at it, you remember me."

"Um." Wind closed the box and set it on the floor between us.

"What's the matter?"

"There's something I need to tell you." Wind told me. "Well, a couple of things, really."

"Um—okay."

"I can't accept this until I tell you—it's about my father's death."

My heart stopped.

I nodded.

"Me not getting to say goodbye to my dad wasn't your fault." Wind told me. "It wasn't your fault."

"I don't—I don't understand."

"Mae told me that my father died right after getting off the phone with me that day." He hung his head. "She said that he called to say goodbye because he knew he wasn't going to make it until I got home. I didn't know."

Tears rolled down his cheeks and that hurt me more than believing I had stolen something from him all those years. Instead of being angry, I wrapped my arms around him and drew him to me. I tried hushing him, but Wind was inconsolable. No matter what I said to him, he just cried harder.

"It's okay." I told him. 'I promise."

"Wind, *kho tod, na*?" He pleaded. "Wind, *kho tod*."

As his tears soaked into my shirt, I simply held onto him tighter.

"There's something else." He shifted from my arms to pull something from his pocket.

He didn't have to tell me what it was. I recognized the envelop.

"Where did you get this?" I asked.

"From Gear. He thought I'd dropped it in the hall."

Closing my eyes, I tried to push away the nerves that now pulsed through me.

"Is this why you—" I looked at him. "Is this why you agreed to being my boyfriend."

"No!" Wind exclaimed. "I agreed because…"

His cheeks flushed.

"I'm your boyfriend because I want to be." Wind pointed out. "You thought I was sexy all this time? And the way you describe me—I can't ever live up to that."

"*Take My Body*—I wrote that because of you, because of the way you made my body feel."

Wind bowed forward and wrapped his arms around me.

"I always wanted you, Wind." I admitted. "Every word I wrote in that letter was—and still is—true."

He sighed and held me tighter.

I didn't know when it happened, but we fell asleep tangled in each other's arms.

Something woke me up a while later and I carried Wind to bed. After a bathroom break, I pulled him to my chest and lifted the sheets up to his shoulders only to go back to sleep.

The next time I woke up, I was alone. I jerked upward in bed and looked around the room.

"Wind?"

I couldn't stop the race of my heart as I untangled myself from the sheets and darted out into the living area of our suite.

Nothing.

"Wind?"

Rushing back into the bedroom, I was in time to see Wind exited the bathroom.

"P?" He asked, confusion written all over his face. "What's the matter?"

"You're here."

"Um—yes. Where else would I be?"

I smiled. "Of course, you're here."

"I ordered breakfast." Wind told me. "But there's something—"

He paused to lift the box with the necklace to me.

"I don't know if you still wanted me to have this."

Without a word, I took the box from his hand, removed the necklace and walked behind him. Lifting it over his head, I hooked it around his neck then turned to look at the heart-shaped pendant.

"I bought it for my boyfriend." My voice hitched.

"And I got you something too." Wind told me.

When he produced a black bag, I accepted it and quickly looked in then laughed. My cheeks exploded with heat as I was only able to laugh harder.

Imagining Wind walking into a store to buy condoms and lube was the most hilarious thing to me.

He smacked my arm and turned to leave.

I caught him around the hips and dropped him on the bed.

"You came prepared, Wind." I placed the bag beside him as I climbed over him. "So, I'll reward you."

He smiled up at me in a way that sent my whole body into a warm glow.

Even if I wanted to resist him then, I couldn't. The pink of his cheeks was one thing but the dare in his eyes caused me to lean back to peel his shirt off.

When I tried doing the same for mine, Wind caught my hands and pushed them away.

Smiling, I lifted my hands above my head and allowed him to undress me. The moment my shirt was off, he was sitting up and kissing my chest and downward to my abs.

"I love your body so much." He whispered.

I sighed.

He nipped at the flesh then leaned up to get my neck and shoulder.

I buried my fingers into his hair, holding his mouth over one nipple. I kissed his forehead then tossed my head back when the desire became too much.

"Wind." I whispered.

He looked up at me.

His eyes told me everything.

Wind was ready.

He wasn't afraid.

From somewhere in my dazed mind, I managed to reach across for the bag and by the time he was on his knees facing away from me, I was so happy I thought I'd burst into tears. I touched him, dragging my fingertips against his perfect skin. It all gave me so much joy, I couldn't remember ever feeling this way.

It was slow going at first—everything I did was by instinct. I knew this first time would be hard on him and the last thing I wanted to do was hurt him.

But though our first time was slow, I didn't mind. I wanted to mark Wind as mine, offer him my body and see if he would accept everything I offered.

His nails dragging down my back brought me to life, made me arch into him.

I allowed him to roll us over and tower above me.
Watching him rise and fall on me casted a kind of
spell over me that I willingly gave in to.

"Storm." Wind whispered against my ear before
his teeth sunk into the flesh.

I growled for him, allowed my body to do things
with him and for him that I never thought I was
capable of. I gave in, letting him play me like a finely
tuned instrument and I proudly sang for him until I
couldn't control it anymore.

He came for me, and my cheeks heated. I held him
tightly against my chest. Wind pressed his face to my
shoulders and I knew why—he was embarrassed.

Laughing softly, I kissed the side of his head, but
he didn't stay that way. He lifted his head to look into
my eyes before lifting his body and reaching down to
grab me.

"You have to let go." I warned through gritted
teeth.

"Why, P?" He asked, stroking me slowly.

"You're going to—"

He smirked, tightened his fist and the whole world
kind of exploded into splinters of light. He caught my
cries of joy in his mouth, in a kiss until we both
toppled backward onto the bed.

"Are you okay?" I asked, lying him on the bed
then pushing to my elbow to look down into his face.

"Stop asking that."

"This was your first time, Wind." I caressed a hand
down his arm then up again to his shoulder. "It's my
first too—I just wanted to make sure I did it right."

"Trust me, P." He turned his face into my chest.
"You did it fine."

"Just fine?" I teased, bowing my head to nuzzle his
neck.

He punched my arm. "P."

I laughed softly.

As our bodies calmed, I exhaled and climbed out of the bed. I walked away with Wind's eye son my body. When I glanced over my shoulder at him, he didn't pretend not to be staring. Smiling, I hauled on my boxers and pants then wandered out into the living room to pull open the fridge. I gathered drinks, dug through my bag for snacks then went back to the room.

The bed was empty.

"Wind?"

"Gimme a minute." Wind replied. "Just need to wash my hands."

I sat on the bed and waited until he walked out again. He was partially dressed—that disappointed me.

"Why is it every time I wake up you're out of my bed?" I asked.

"Blame my bladder, P."

I laughed, took his hand and helped him back into bed. We snacked—I kept asking if he was sore.

Wind frowned at me.

For the first time, I went on dates with my partner. We had breakfast together, alone in a beautiful dining room. Then we joined Bank and Pretty for snacks and time to hang out. We saw in the water for a while and eventually, Pretty left us to go meet with her boyfriend. The rest of us sat, exhausted in the sand, staring outward at the dying sun.

We all sat there silently, the temperature cooling around us, breathing softly.

"Are you happy, Wind?" Bank asked. "Because that's important, you know?"

I turned to look at Wind who was smiling and staring out over the dying sun. The answer to that question was important to me—it was scary how important that question was to me.

"Yes." Wind replied. "I'm very happy."

He rested his forehead to my shoulder.

The room erupting in cheers as my character held Wind's against the wall and kissed him. My cheeks flushed and Wind reached over to squeeze my hand.

When someone cat-called from the back, Wind pressed his face into my shoulder but all I could do was grin proudly.

Seua had set up a preview of the movie for the cast and crew. As it played, I couldn't remember ever feeling so proud of anything—ever.

When the movie ended, everyone cheered. Kai, Wind, Bank, Gear and I rallied around to hug Seua until he squealed happily.

"And can we talk about the music?" Bank asked. "I need those songs on my playlist. *My Heartbeat* is my favourite."

"Mine too!" Wind sighed.

"But you have the singer right here." Bank grinned. "He can sing it for you any time you want."

Wind blushed. "You suck."

"I know!" Bank grinned.

"Seriously, Bank's got a point." Kai pointed. "You know they're going to be looking for those on the *Base Note* song list."

"Have you guys given any thoughts to a soundtrack?" Wind asked.

Kai, Seua and I exchanged glances.

"You have an idea there." I kissed Wind.

"But for tonight." Seua said. "Can we not think about it? Can we just celebrate surviving the making of the movie?"

We all agreed and went back to the party.

Wind left me to use the bathroom and when he came back, he stopped at the snack table.

As he ate, he fed me from his plate.

The girls around us giggled each time I took something from his fingers with my mouth and I knew what was going to happen.

The pictures would be online soon enough.

I sighed.

As the party ended, we all figured out how we were going to head home.

I paused to hug Seua.

"Listen, I have a gift for you." I told him while rummaging into my pocket for the keys to my Bentley. Over the past few weeks, I'd had it repainted.

"I can't." Seua told me.

"Yes, you can." I told him. "You put up with a lot over the last little while. And your car is basically done. It would cost more to fix that thing."

"But Storm—it's a Bentley."

"It would do more good with you driving it than sitting in some garage gathering dust." I pointed out. "You're my brother. What's mine is yours. That's how it works."

"Have you spoken to Wind about this?" Seua asked. "What does he think? I mean, you could give him this car."

I smirked. "I like driving my man around."

Seua blushed but took the key.

"It's at Gear's house." I told him. "When you can, get Kai to ride you over there to get it. All the paperwork has been done."

Seua hugged me tightly. "I don't know how I come to deserve a friend like you."

"I'm pretty sure that's not how it works." I laughed. "But for all you do for me, for *Base Note* and you never asked for anything. You have to understand, that when you're good to people, they tend to want to be good to you back."

"So, what you're saying is to stop being good to people?" He smirked.

I grinned. "Go. Bank is waiting for you."

Seua hugged me again then took off jogging toward where Bank was waiting in his Ferrari.

Wind

It didn't take much convincing to get all the guys together. When I ran the idea by my mother, she was so excited, she went to her best friend and gathered as much bamboo sprouts as she could get.

When she asked for time off to spend with us, her boss refused.

My mother quit.

I knew she was worried about what she would do after we went away again. But when I spoke with her the night before, she'd told me not to worry.

How could I not worry?

But for the moment, I would be strong. If she saw my sadness, she wouldn't enjoy the time we wanted to spend with her.

Before we left the city, Storm and I stopped at the grocery store and stocked up. We then climbed onto the private bus Kai hired and it took us into my village.

We all descended on Mae's house. Gear, Storm and I slept in the same room. Bank, Kai and Seua slept in the living room.

No one complained.

I thought my mother would have been overwhelmed, but as she interacted with my friends, she was absolutely glowing. In no time at all, she had them all calling her Mae and she giggled every time they did. She took a particular liking to Gear—maybe it was because he was around my age.

The plan was, we'd all spend a week with Mae, then they would all leave me there.

What my mother didn't know was that I had a surprise for her. I'd called in a favour with Bank's father, a favour the man didn't even think twice about granting.

"Have you told her?" Bank asked.

"Told me what?" Mae wanted to know.

"Give us a minute?" I asked Bank.

He tapped my shoulder and exited through the back door and down into the backyard with the others.

I cleared my throat and moved to stand beside my mother as she peeled some sweet potatos.

"Mae, if I can get you a new job, better pay, better hours, less stress on your—but you'd have to move from this village back to the city."

"Closer to you?"

"A bus ride." I replied. "Would you take it?"

"Depends on the job."

"Bank's father owns a hotel—it's called *The Golden Butterfly*."

"Wait—his father owns that?" Mae asked.

I nodded. "I spoke to his dad about you, and your years in the business. And he's looking to offer you a job."

"What kind?"

"Head of housekeeping." I replied. "The man who had the job is moving to England to be with his daughter and grandson."

"I would need a place to stay until my first pay."

"Don't worry about that." I told her proudly. "Storm's grandfather has a small house close by. No one has used it for a few years. He said you're welcomed to it until you can find your own place."

Tears rolled down her cheeks and I couldn't help but hug her.

"What's wrong, Mae?" I asked. "I don't want you livings so far and working so hard anymore. I always want what's best for you, what makes you happy."

"I'm happy." She assured me. "My son went away and came back to take care of me. That's what every mother hopes. But you've made some amazing friends, my love."

She leaned back to frame my face.

"You'll take this help?" I asked her.

"Of course." She kissed both my cheeks then my forehead. "I think I need to find a way to thank N'Bank's father. Maybe I can bake something."

I laughed. "You'll figure it out. We'll take you into the city to meet with him in a few days."

"But for right now, I have myboys!" She squealed happily.

"Oh, no." I groaned.

Mae kissed my nose. "Go out back with the others."

"You don't need any help?"

"Boy, don't make me tell you again."

I giggled, kissed her cheek before hurrying over to the fridge. I gathered some juice for all of us and did as she said. There wasn't any extra chairs so I sat in Storm's lap.

They were all happy that Mae accepted the job. Bank immediately called his father. The two had a talk and the meeting between his father and my mother was set.

For the first time, I sat around, enjoying laughter and people. Storm and Kai had brought their guitar and the night air filled with music. Storm sang for us, Gear snapped pictures of everything and Bank tried singing a few songs from *Base Note*. Granted, his voice wasn't as good at Storm's or Kai's but Bank could hold his own.

As a matter of fact, he rapped so good, Seua's jaw dropped.

Mae was happy with us, she laughed louder than I'd heard her laugh since my father's death. Kai stocked a plate of food for her and she touched his head as he served her.

He grinned proudly.

After the food was gone, Seua whipped out the desserts we'd brought. He ensured Mae had the mung bean candies and Mae's face lit up.

As the evening passed into night, we gave her the night off. While she showered, all of us mulled around to clean up the kitchen and the backyard.

We bathed in the swimming hole, and when the night finally settled, Storm and I camped in the backyard giving Kai and Gear my bed.

I didn't mind.

Storm wrapped me in his arms but I couldn't settle. Instead, I turned my head to kiss his neck then his shoulder.

"Storm?"

"Mmm?"

"I want you…"

"Now?" Storm asked.

When I nodded, Storm closed the tent and rolled us over so that he hovered over me. He didn't question me further and when he kissed me, I realized how much I'd missed his lips on mine.

I'd wanted this all day, all through the laughter and the food. All through the hugs and the beautiful atmosphere, I'd missed his kiss, his hands grabbing my thigh to open me up to him.

He nibbled at my neck my shoulder until somehow we were both sitting up and peeling each other's shirts off.

Storm whorshipped my body, touching me, tasting at me.

"Storm." I sighed, catching his earlobe between my teeth.

When I reached down to grab him, Storm caught my wrist and pulled my hand away.

"We don't have—"

I fumbled around to my bag and pulled out the golden packet and held it out to him.

Storm smirked, kissed me and accepted it. "I love your preparedness."

"I've been thinking about this all day." I admitted.

Storm kissed me then made his way down my body.

He made me burn for him—even as he plunged into me and I dug my nails into his back.

"Wind." Storm sighed, arching backward.

He flipped us over and I braced my palms to his bare chest and rolled my hips for him.

This time, when everything fell apart, he sat up to catched my cries of happiness into his mouth.

It didn't even cross my mind to hold it in, or people would come rushing out to check on us.

Storm did that to me.

He made me mindless with pleasure—he made me not afraid.

By the time we slumped together in the tent, I could barely breathe but my body was happy.

I was happy.

Storm groaned. "Are you okay?"

"Okay *khrap*."

"The ground isn't very soft, I didn't want—"

"I'm okay." I assured him. "Right now I'm trying to learn how to breathe again. You did that to me."

Storm laughed softly. "You remember when you said that I couldn't be that good of a lover?"

My cheeks flushed even more. I remembered the day perfectly. Clearing my throat then licking my lips, I sighed.

"Mm." I ~~relplied.~~ replied

"Have I proven myself?" Storm asked.

I laughed.

He rolled over to nuzzle my neck. "What's your answer?"

I sighed and reached down to touch him. "You've proven yourself."

Storm laughed happily and scooped me into his arms, hauling me ontop of him. He nuzzled my ~~throgh~~ throat then moved his head to kiss me deeply.

"Storm?" I called to him when we settled into the night again.

"Mm?"

"You do really love me, right?" I asked. "I mean, I don't think I could handle it if this was just a phase you were going through."

Storm pushed to his elbow and caught my chin between his thumb and forefinger. "I've been through those thoughts. I've had to ask myself that question. I've had time to find the answer and be okay with it."

I sighed—the seriousness in his eyes took my breath away.

"I do love you, Wind." His voice cracked. "I think I've loved you since the moment I wrote that letter. That day after you barged into my house and yelled at me, I should have been angry. But all I felt was this—warmth in me that only you've been able to make me feel."

"You don't have to—"

"I have to." Storm kissed my lips gently. "I need you to be confident in our relationship. I need you to walk around with your ~~hold~~ head held proudly because I'm your man."

I knelt over him. Staring down into his eyes in the dimly lit space made me happy. Framing his face, I leaned forward so I was close to him.

"I'm proud you're mine." I admitted. "But sometimes you're going to have to remind me that I'm yours."

"And how exactly would you like that reminder?" I teased.

"With your body." I giggled.

Storm laughed. "But I do love you, Wind."

"I love you too…" I sighed, kissed him and rolled off him to cuddle him.

"Let's get some sleep." Storm told me. "We should open the tent to get some air in."

I nodded.

Storm

The sound of the night was musical around me as I stood by the door, watching Wind on the balcony. He was watching the moon travel across the sky, the reflection of it against the water. Unable to stop myself, I walked up behind him, wrapped my arms around him and rested my chin on his shoulder.

"Papa says hello." I told him.

"Mmm."

No other words passed between us for a silent forever. Eventually, Wind turned in the enclosure of my arms, leaned his back against the rail and looked into my eyes. I wasn't sure what he was searching for, but he stared at me, a small smile on his face.

"P…"

"After what we did to each other?" I asked.

He hung his head.

"No, you don't." I teased, using my thumb to lift his chin. "You can't be shy in this moment. Now, call me, Storm."

"But, P…"

"You're my lover." I pointed out. "You're allowed to be formal with me."

He sighed. "Okay—Storm."

I moaned. "I actually love it when you say my name." Wind blushed. "Stom…"

He rested a hand to my chest.

"I wanted to tell you something." Wind touched my cheek then dropped his hand. "I think you deserve to hear me say this."

I tilted my head. "You don't have to tell me I'm sexy."

"P'Storm!"

I laughed.

"Be serious for a second."

"Okay, my love." I kissed his lips playfully. "You have my complete and undivided attention."

"This is a little important—well, it's very important and I don't want to regret not saying this to you." Wind's shoulders rose and fell heavily. "I love you."

"Um…this isn't because of the letter, right?" Storm asked. "You weren't ever supposed to see that. I went into the box, and I guess I must have crapped it—"

"It's not about the damn letter!" He ducked under my arm and was running.

I caught his arm and pulled him back.

"What's this?" I asked.

"You didn't want to hear that." He hung his head. "I should have waited longer, right?"

I watched him, the way he fidgeted and wasn't able to hold my gaze. He tried getting away from me by pulling his arm from my grasp I held onto him, even pulling him into my chest and wrapping my arms around him. I kissed his neck and cheek and head.

"Say something." Wind sobbed. "It's just hanging on the air like a bad smell, and I can't take it back."

"Why would you take it back?"

"Well, you like me enough." Wind stepped back. "I know you like me. But I just changed this entire situation. Even if you don't love me—I love you. That's the only reason I allowed—well, the only reason I made love with you."

"I love you too."

"Really?"

I framed his cheeks and pressed my forehead to his. "I've loved you since the day you barged into my house and told off. It may not seem like it, but I did everything I could to get you to notice me."

Wind closed his eyes. "The scholarship."

"Don't be angry." I held him tighter. "The thought of you hurting because you couldn't go to school—the thought of you crying—I couldn't…"

The words died in my throat, threatening to choke me.

"I couldn't live with that—please understand I did it not to buy you or anything like that." I stepped away. "I did it because I wanted to see you smile."

Wind sighed.

I could see the wheels cranking inside his head.

"Being my roommate."

I nodded.

"I was wondering why a senior was my roommate." He told me. "I probably should be angry at you. But no one has cared for me enough to go this out of their way for me."

"You're not angry?"

"I'm crossed with you." Wind told me, poking a finger not my chest.

"What's my punishment?"

Wind turned his back to me and stared out over at the view. I palmed his shoulders and caressed them then down his back.

"I won't make love to you for a week." Wind announced.

My heart sank. "That's a little severe, don't you think?"

"What you did was severe." Wind looked up into my face. "Right?"

"I did it out of love." I pointed out. "This is torture."

Wind frowned at me.

"I love your body." I stepped closer and kissed his neck. "The way you blush when I get naked for you. How am I going to go a week without that?"

"Then you should have thought about it before you did what you did."

I groaned and continue nuzzling his neck.

"Baby…"

Wind sighed and faced me. "Just—don't do things like this again, okay? If you want to do something nice for me, talk to me."

"What if I want to surprise you?"

Wind eyed me. "You can take me out for noodles."

"Buy you flowers?"

He smiled. "Take me to the beach—take me for a ride—take me to see Mae."

"You're not asking for much."

"I'm simple, P." He admitted. "I mean, Storm. All I really need from you is love."

"And my body?"

Wind blushed. "And your body."

"You're shameless." I teased.

"Only with you." He replied. "And is there something wrong with wanting to be naughty for my boyfriend?" Wind wanted to know, coyly.

"Mmm." I Smiled. "No, in fact, I encourage it. But call me that again."

"Call you what?"

"You called me *my boyfriend*."

"That's what you are, right?" Wind asked. "My boyfriend.

He kissed my cheek and darted into the bedroom through the glass door. I turned to see the curtains blowing in the wind and I couldn't stop the smile to grace my lips.

As I stood there, staring after him, I knew then I'd found the love of my life.

Grinning, I followed him into the room to see him sitting on the bed with both our towels. I leaned against the doorframe as he smiled at me.

"Shower with me?" Wind tossed my towel at me.

I caught it. "I thought I was on punishment."

"If you'd rather go on drought for a week, we can do that too." Wind told me.

I rushed over and scooped him into my arms. He squealed happily and tangled his arms around my neck.

"You love me, Sunan Rattanakasin." My voice cracked around the kisses.

"And you love me too, Klahan Bannarasee."

The End

More from SusuKhaa

King and Dom

King's life is a prison, controlled by his father. It wasn't his and he's learned to put his head down and do as he's told. When he's forced to move to Canada to take over one of his father's hotel, King meets Dom, and for the first time ever, King is beginning to realize, there is more to life than his father's orders.

After his father's death, Dom's life has been slowly spiraling out of control. Working as freelance security, he's hired to drive King around and keep him safe. But when danger begins lurking around every corner, Dom will have some tough decisions to make.

www.amazon.com/King-Dom-Susu-Khaa-ebook/dp/B093GQ879

Printed in Great Britain
by Amazon